I0664875

THE CHRONICLE OF T'NARG

Grant Burgess

This is a work of fiction. Names, characters, places, and incidents either are the product of the author's imagination or are used fictitiously, and any resemblance to actual persons, living or dead, businesses, companies, events, or locales is entirely coincidental.

Published by Snowflake Publishing. P.O. Box 6662, Moore, Oklahoma 73153-0662,USA www.snowflakepublishing.net

ISBN 978-0-9821798-0-2

Printed in the United States of America

Foreword

The first time I met the author, or should I say the one to whom I gave this chronicle, was in 1974, just months after he had turned 16. This chronicle was given to him on a single parchment of deer skin, and had been time sealed until 1988 when he would turn 30. At that time, the seal would dissolve and its contents were to be copied into the English language and published. This was all supposed to have been finished and published by the early 1990's, but for reasons not given to me, it was not going to be published until after the turn of the 21st century.

As a watcher, I know that everything that happens will happen according to plan and at the exact time and order in which it needs to happen. So why it is being published now, instead of in 1988, I do not know, but I do know it is by design, and therefore must be for the best.

One of the results of this being published at a later date, is that some of the events described in the chronicle have already occurred, so that the reader may have a greater appreciation and understanding of future events. Also, the symbiotic nature of all the events and ideologies happening in the present time begin to make much more sense when seen as a whole.

The nature of the parchment which was given to the author, which he will describe in his introduction, was of a technology which isn't present today, but there was a specific time frame of six months in which to translate the document. After that period of time, the writing would disappear, and be lost for all eternity. However, the document was translated and written down, but as stated before, the reasons for the delay were not revealed to me.

Because of the responsibilities and nature of the remaining watchers, it is not our duty to keep track on the affairs of individual humans, and when we do have contact, it is on a one time basis, after which we are no longer to have contact with them. Therefore I found it very strange when I was once again instructed to meet with the author and give him more forceful and persuasive reasons to publish the chronicle. As you can see, since you are reading this, it has been published, and the document is now legally in force as a testimony to mankind. What this means will be explained more in the chronicle. It has been said by our Creator that, " to whom much has been given, much is required" so read this and be wise.

T'narg

INTRODUCTION

How do you convince an audience that what you are saying is true, when if you had not experienced the event, you wouldn't believe it either? I really don't know, but will present everything to the reader and let them decide for themselves. I did not ask for this, nor do I have a good reason as to why I had to be the one to go through the ordeal of having it published and then promoting it.

Its been nearly twenty years since I first read and wrote down the chronicle, and it still seems to far fetched to be true. There is no evidence remaining of what I had been given, as will be explained, and the only thing remaining is the deer hide it was written on, and anyone could purchase or get possession of a deer skin if they wanted one.

Therefore, I present this work as a piece of fiction, and will not try to convince anyone otherwise. So I ask the reader to be entertained by this, or to take it as a forewarning. In either case may you be enriched by it.

GRANT BURGESS

CHAPTER ONE

How can I explain the delay of releasing this story, or chronicle, except to say that besides being lazy, I sometimes find the circumstances involved in receiving this testament not only incredulous, but have reservations myself as to the veracity of its contents. I must admit that the events foretold to the present have been accurate, so perhaps it is my perception of what people will think that has kept me from having it published. After all, why should anyone listen to an unknown author who is simply relaying a message that was given to him many years ago?

Many of the questions I had were answered in the first part of the chronicle, such as "why me," and "what is this," and I know the reader will have many of the same questions I had, so I will let the document explain itself. For now, let me just explain the circumstances of how I came to be in possession of it.

It was in mid-November of 1974, and I was on my first real

elk hunt. Every year at this time, several family members and friends would get together and go hunting in the far northeast corner of Oregon. I had been going to these gathering since I was twelve, but this was the first time that I would legally be able to hunt.

Now every year we set camp in the same spot, so everyone was familiar with the area, and no one went out alone unless they had been there at least once before. Since I had been there several years, I knew the area very well, and had spent the last two years extensively searching certain nearby hills and valleys in anticipation of when I would be able to hunt on my own. I have a natural sense of direction, and having explored the area, the events that unfolded that day have always been a mystery to me.

No one got much sleep the night before, for as usual, after dinner the talk turned to stories of previous hunts, and of trophies taken and of those that had gotten away. As always, the stories seemed to get better every year, but no one seemed to mind hearing them again, and we all bedded down, thinking about that big bull elk that we were going to get.

We woke early that Thursday morning (elk hunting was one of those few things that you could be excused from school for) to find a light coat of snow on everything. This wasn't particularly unusual for this time of year, being in the mountains and all, but everyone hoped that more was not on the way. We got up early, maybe 5:00 a.m., but someone had already gotten up and stoked the campfire, and had eggs and bacon waiting. I still wonder if some of them ever went to bed, but I was grateful, for the only thing harder than getting up early, is to get up that early cold and hungry.

It didn't take long to eat, and by time we left camp that morning, the snow had stopped, the clouds had cleared away, and the thousands if not millions of stars that can be seen when one is away from civilization, were twinkling to one another as if to signal the end of another night. Within thirty minutes, the day was dawning and most of us had left camp to get to our own particular site, some of which were several miles away. No one had horses, and it was before 4-wheelers became popular for hunting, so for convenience sake, most of us tried to stay within a couple of miles. If anyone has had to dress, pack out, or help finish packing out a large bull elk, you know exactly what I'm talking about.

The previous year, I had found a short but steep ravine about a mile north of camp, and had planned on getting there around mid morning, but was first going to walk through a meadow about half a mile west of camp where we had seen some elk the day before.

The dirt road that we came in on every year was about 60 miles from the state highway, and we would camp at the end of this road every year. At the end of this road, it made a large circle (perhaps a half mile or less) back onto itself, so that any large vehicles would not have to turn around, but could continue on the road unimpaired, and it was this loop that was to be my undoing that day, as I shall explain.

We always camped on the east side of the road, about half way around the loop, so if one traveled due west a few hundred feet, you would cross the west side of the road, and just west of that was the meadow where I was going to. I arrived at the meadow just as the sun was coming up, and was thrilled to see several elk there. The meadow was a pasture of green grass, and although it was a natural pasture, it was so picturesque it seemed as if it had been purposefully planted there. Unfortunately, all I saw were cow elk, but still I stayed there for about an hour in case any bulls might show up. They didn't, so I headed back the way I came, so I could get to my ravine while it was still early.

Now instead of just following my own tracks back, I thought I could take a shortcut, which ended up in my getting lost. I crossed the road, knowing that I would cross the other part of the road fairly quickly, but after about thirty minutes of not reaching the road, I knew something was wrong. I wandered around trying to find the other part of the road, but after about an hour, I knew it was useless. By now, it had started warming up, and what little snow was left had started melting, so there was no use in trying to backtrack. About a mile away I could see the top of a large hill, and thinking I recognized it, I decided to get to the top of it, so I could perhaps get my bearings.

I don't know how far it actually was, but it took me almost two hours to get to the top of it, so it must have been much further than a mile. Unfortunately I did not recognize anything when I got to the top, but what was on the other side was seemingly hopeful. Far off in the distance, was a road, and because of the river running along side of it, I knew it wasn't the road we came in on, but I did know that I could probably follow it to the state highway and then come back up on the road we camped on. I knew that I could probably catch a ride with someone if they were going that way, and at the time, didn't realize how naïve this was.

From the top of the hill, or mountain, there was a steep valley that flowed to the southeast, and this was the path that I would have to take to reach the road. It would have been much quicker to go straight eastward, but it was surrounded by cliffs, and looked to be not only difficult, but maybe impossible. I also noticed about halfway down the first path, a creek, and this was encouraging, for by this time I was starting to get hot and thirsty.

I sat at the top for a few more minutes, and was just getting ready to descend, when I noticed that a jeep had pulled up and stopped at the end of the ravine, and that a man had gotten out and was looking over something that from this distance I thought looked like a map. This thrilled me, and I started going down the hill as fast as I could. Now even though there wasn't much brush in the way to hinder my progress, there was some, and by time I reached the creek halfway down the mountain, I was exhausted and thirsty. The water was coming out of the mountain, probably fed by a snow spring, and was very cold, but at the same time refreshing. I didn't have a watch, but I probably spent ten or fifteen minutes recovering before finally continuing on, and after what seemed like an eternity I finally made it to the road, and the man and his vehicle were still there. Now at the time, I didn't think there was anything strange about this, but looking back on it, I realize that for someone to have stayed at that same location for that length of time was very strange, very strange indeed.

CHAPTER 2

When I had almost reached the bottom of the valley where the man in the jeep was, I became very anxious, thinking he might leave, so for about the last quarter of a mile, I was running as fast as I could. I was tired, hungry, and the rifle I was carrying seemed like it weighed a hundred pounds, so by time I reached the bottom of the ravine, I was having a hard time catching my breath.

" What are you in such a hurry about out here in the middle of nowhere," the stranger asked smilingly. " You act like somebody is chasing you or something."

" No" I gasped out, " I was trying to get down this hill before you left, and I was just hurrying."

" Well," the stranger replied, " I'm not in near as big of hurry as you are, so rest a second, and tell me why the rush."

At the time, it struck me as a little odd, that the man's skin was so pale, so pale in fact that I didn't know how he kept from getting sunburned from just being outside, and although it wasn't particularly hot out, and there weren't any clouds, the rays of the sun beating down full force made it seem hotter than it really was. I guess the straw hat he had on gave him all the protection he needed, and though I would have thought a hunter would have had a different kind of hat, I didn't really give it much thought at the time. Other than that, he looked pretty ordinary, probably in his forties judging by the little bit of gray in his sideburns. He was thin, but not skinny, and probably just under six feet tall. Now the eyes were a different story. If anything was stranger than his pale skin, it was those eyes. It wasn't scary, or freakish, but they had a dark blackness to them, so much so that you had a hard time seeing any white. They were a little bigger than normal, and somewhat almond shaped. I kept trying to get a really good look at them, but between his hat shading his eyes, and not wanting to be rude and stare, I couldn't tell much more than that.

It had been quite a while since I had drank from the stream, and I was starting to feel the dryness of my throat again, when as if reading my mind he nodded over to the side of the jeep, and said, " you look a little thirsty. There is a canteen full of water on the passenger seat, help yourself."

" Thanks," I said as I got up from the side of the road where I had been sitting. The window was down, so I reached in and got the canteen, and took a nice long drink from it. Thirst has a way of making even something as simple as water taste excellent and this was no exception. " Thanks again," I said after taking a couple of more sips from the canteen and putting it back in the jeep. " That really hit the spot."

" Glad to be of help," he answered, " so what were you in such a hurry about?"

" Well, I got lost, and I was on the top of that mountain right there when I saw you stop on the side of the road, and I figured you might be able to help me out. The closer to the road I got, the more worried I was that you might drive off, so that's why I started running."

For the first time, it dawned on me that it probably had taken quite a while to descend, and it was eerie that he hadn't driven off. I didn't have a watch on me, and since it was early when I got lost, and judging by the position of the sun, it was probably around noon, or at least early afternoon, it must have taken quite a while. But any anxiety I may have had was quickly relieved when the stranger reached inside the jeep and pulled out a map.

" Lets see if we can find out where we are, and where you need to get back to," he said. " I've got some type of map here that used to be used by miners and surveyors, so I think we can figure out something."

It didn't take long to find out where we were, I just found the town where the road we camped on originated, and then followed it to the end. The only problem was, that the road I was on now was definitely not the same one. They both had their head in the same town, but since they ran parallel to one another, or nearly parallel, it was only six or seven miles from the road I was on now, to the one we camped on.

" If your headed back to town, I could catch a ride with you, then maybe find someone coming back on the other road," I said hopefully. I knew it would be to much to ask if the stranger would go that far out of his way to bring me back, but I was thinking he might volunteer to.

" That's one way of going about it, and I am headed back that way, but what are you going to do if there is no one to give you a ride back out this way?" he said. " Its nearly fifty miles each way, and there isn't anyway you can get back to your camp today if you have to walk that far. Not to mention that everyone will be worried about you if your not back by dark, but looking at this map, I think there is a better way. About half a mile north of here, there is a creek that goes from this road all the way to the road you are camped on."

" How far do you think it is?" I asked.

" Well it looks to be six miles give or take a little, and that would get you back just about dark."

I remembered that there was a creek not to far from camp, and after taking a good look at the map, realized that it had to be the same one. " I think you are right, and that would be the best way to go. Would you mind to much giving me a ride to the creek?" I queried.

" Not at all, hop in and we can go there now."

We spent the next few minutes turning around and driving to the creek in silence, and all I could think of was how nice it was going to be to get back to camp, and although it was going to take a while to walk back, and I was already tired, it was a relief to know I wasn't lost anymore.

" Wake up, we're here." The strangers voice startled me, and I couldn't believe that I had fallen asleep in the five minutes it had taken to get to the creek. " Here, take my canteen, because it doesn't look like this creek has any water in it, and your going to need it by time you get done walking."

" Are you sure?" I asked. " You've really helped me out today, and there is no way I can repay you for all this help,"

" That's not a problem," he said. " As you get older you will realize that the best help you can give someone, is the kind that they cannot repay. Not that you want them to feel indebted to you, but it's a type of charity that brings great blessings to you."

" Well, I appreciate it very much," I said as I got out of the jeep and slung my rifle over one shoulder. I took a quick drink from the canteen, then strapped it over the other shoulder and prepared for the walk back to camp. " Thanks again," I repeated as I started toward the creek, " You've really helped me out."

There was a culvert underneath the road so there wouldn't be any severe damage in the spring when the creek would be full from the melting winter snows, and I had just gotten past that when the stranger hollered at me. " Hey wait, I have something I need to give to you."

" That's okay, you've given more than enough help today," I replied.

" No, this is something that I have to give to you. Its why I waited so long for you to come down the mountain. It took you almost three hours to get all the way down. Doesn't it strike you a little odd that I stayed there all that time?"

It had crossed my mind briefly before, but I had quickly forgotten it because of the relief of knowing I wasn't lost anymore, and that there was someone to help. Nothing like this had every happened to me, or to anyone that I knew of, and I was starting to get that spooky feeling again, when as if reading my mind again, he said. " Don't be alarmed, everything is fine, and there is nothing to be scared or upset about. Let me introduce myself properly. My name is T'narg, (pronounced Narg) and I have been sent here to give you this chronicle that I've written."

His voice had a soothing effect, and though I was still bewildered, I didn't have any fears like I did just moments before. It didn't take long for him to open up the back of the jeep, and to pull out a box covered in newspaper. He carefully tore the newspaper off, and opened the box. Inside was a deer hide neatly folded, with some type of golden medallion on it, which he carefully pulled out and handed to me.

" This is what we have always written our chronicles on, the skin or hide of animals. It keeps much better than any other type of material, and is not heavy or bulky like stone. Once you read it, you will understand this a lot better, so I'm not going to explain it all now. You said you wanted a way to repay me, and this is the way. I will explain all that is necessary for you to know now, then you need to get going, because you need to get back to your camp before it gets dark."

T'narg put the hide back into the box and handed it to me, but did not put the lid back on. It was much lighter than I imagined it was going to be, almost as if nothing was in the box at all. " See that gold medallion on top of the skin?" he asked. Then without waiting for a reply he continued on. " That is a time seal made out of a metal which you have never heard of, and even though it looks like gold, its much more valuable. It is of such a hardness, that nothing can break it, and once this metal has been molded no heat can destroy it. However, they are designed to disintegrate at a predetermined time, so they make the perfect seal."

By now, I figured this guy was crazy or something, but I thought it best to humor him, and get going as soon as I could. " I know what your thinking," he said, " but everything that I am telling you is true, as you will find out in due time. I want you to listen carefully to the instructions I'm going to give you, because if you forget them, everything will be for naught.

When you turn thirty, this seal will disintegrate, and you will be able to read the chronicle that I have written inside. Do not try and break the seal, and above all else, do not cut the hide in an attempt to see what is inside. The writing is written in such a way, that it is not visible until the seal breaks up, and it is the chemicals inside the seal that will reveal the writing. I guess you could say it's a type of invisible ink, but its much more complicated than that. If you cut the hide and it is exposed directly to air, the writing will never appear, so please don't do that. Once the seal is gone you can unfold the skin, and read what is there. You are going to have hundreds of questions between now and then, but just know that they will be answered at that time.

It is going to be written in a language that has not been heard on earth since time began, but you will be given the ability to translate it, so that you can write down what you have read. You must be diligent and do it quickly, for it will only stay visible for six months, then the writing will disappear and it will just be an ordinary deer hide.

Then I want you to take what you have written down, and have it published, so that others in the world will be able to share in the knowledge which I am giving you. I can see you are puzzled and scared, but don't be. Everything will be answered in time."

Then without saying another word, this strange man put the lid back on the box, got in his jeep and drove off, leaving me dumbfounded as to what had just transpired. I waited until I saw him disappear around the first corner, than took off running up the creek, not wanting to take the chance that he might come back. I didn't know who he was, but he had definitely given me a scare.

CHAPTER 3

I kept running for what seemed to be at least fifteen minutes and was out of breath and panting, and had no choice but to stop and rest. There was a large smooth rock next to the creek bed, so I sat down on it, and gave myself a chance to think, not only about what had just transpired, but if I should tell anyone about it or not. Having been on a cross country running team for a while must have helped, because in no time I was breathing normal again, and that seemed to have a calming effect so that I could think much more clearly.

There were only a few trees near the creek when I had first started running, but the further I went, the thicker they became, so that by now, perhaps only a mile up the hill the creek came down, it had formed a canopy. It was still early afternoon, but the canopy was thick enough to keep any direct sunlight from coming in, so it seemed later than it really was, and though one could see clearly enough to get around, it was dark. It was much like it is just before a large thunderstorm lets loose its fury; dark and quiet.

The creek didn't vary much in width, but seemed to stay in that three to four foot range for as far as you could see, and even though there wasn't much light, you could still see to the next bend of the creek, so it would be easy to follow. Now and then you would see a pool of water, but except for that, the creek was completely dry, and judging by the well worn path on each side of the creek, plenty of animals came down the mountain this way on their journey to the river. However, the brush and undergrowth was so thick on each side of the creek beyond these paths, that you couldn't see much further than about ten feet on either side.

Probably the only disconcerting thing was how quiet it was. Normally you could hear birds chirping, or insects buzzing around, but here along this creek, it was unnaturally quiet, you couldn't even hear the wind blowing through the trees.

I sat on the rock for a few more minutes then got up and started walking back towards camp. I decided that it was probably best to tell someone what had happened, most likely my dad, just in case something else weird happened, and it wasn't to much longer before I started to hear the normal noises of the birds and bugs again, so it had a calming effect on me, and the fear I had eased out of my mind.

Suddenly, I heard some branches breaking to my side, but when I looked I couldn't see anything because of the brush, and I could feel the goose bumps on my arm appearing. Deep down I knew it was probably a deer or an elk, but I didn't want to find out different, and so I started walking faster up the creek. All thoughts of killing my first elk had completely disappeared from my mind, and the only thing I wanted to do was to be back at camp.

After what seemed like an eternity, I finally made it back to our campground, and none to soon. The sun had gone down, and though it was still light, another ten minutes and it would have been dark. Everyone wondered where I had been, and some thought I might have bagged an elk since it was taking me so long to get back, but I said no, and left it at that. It would have been to embarrassing to let them know I had got lost, so I just told them I had walked further than I thought, and had lost track of the time.

I had every intention of telling my dad what had transpired that day, how I got lost and then the encounter with the stranger known as T'narg, but for some odd reason I couldn't. Everything within me wanted to let him know, but whenever I started to tell him, it wasn't possible. It wasn't until years later when I read the chronicle, that it was revealed how those who have encounters with watchers cannot tell anyone until the proper time. There were a couple of people who wanted to know what was in the box that I had found, but I just told them I had found a deer hide that someone must have lost, so except for that, no one knew what had truly transpired.

The next couple of days went by quickly, but I had lost all interest in hunting. I still went out every morning, as if to hunt, but I stayed as close to camp as I could without raising any suspicions, and spent most of those days just walking around. I didn't really think that the stranger would come back, but I wasn't taking any chances, and wanted to be able to run back if need be.

Finally the week ended and we headed home. I couldn't wait to get back home for a couple of reasons. One, I wanted to get as far away from the area as I could in case the stranger came back, but more importantly, my fear had somewhat subsided, and I wanted to take a closer look at that deer skin. Several times I had started to take it out of the box and examine it further, but someone always seemed to be around, and I knew if anyone saw that medallion or seal, there would be questions that I didn't want to answer.

It was only a couple of days after we got back until I had that chance to really look at it. Everyone had gone grocery shopping, so it was the perfect opportunity. I opened up the box and took out the hide, and looked at the seal more closely. It was gold colored, and about the size of a silver dollar, except that it was about three times thicker. It had something etched on it, but it was hard to tell if it was writing or just scribbling. It seemed to be all jumbled together, and when I looked at it with a magnifying glass it didn't seem to help any. Being the typical teenager, I didn't want to listen to what I had been told, and thought I could break the seal, but it didn't take many hits with a hammer to realize that it wasn't going to break. Not only did it not break, but it didn't even scratch the seal. Even trying to scratch it with a pocketknife didn't do anything, so I gave up on trying to get a better look inside the hide. It did cross my mind to cut off the seal, but something within me knew that if I did that, it would ruin whatever might be inside, so I left it alone.

Those first few months that I had the deer hide, or chronicle which I shall now call it, I must have looked at it nearly everyday, but as time went on, the mystery seemed to ebb and it gradually lost its charm and excitement. Life goes on so they say, and so did the years. After high school I moved to another state to attend college, and between social activities and school studies the thoughts of the chronicle never really entered my mind. You would think that something that odd would have your daily attention, knowing that it was an event that doesn't happen to anyone else, or at least you don't hear about it, but I truly had dismissed it as an event of the past. That's not to say that I didn't ever think about it or look at it, but it was rare that I did, and usually it was because I was moving and had to pack it up, but other than that it was just another one of those things that we store in the closet and call keepsakes.

Eventually I finished school, got married and started working. You could say I didn't finish school since I was a few hours short of a degree, but a business opportunity presented itself, and so I took it. During that time my wife stumbled across the deer hide and wondered what it was, but it was easy to shrug it off and just say it was one of those things that I had before we had met, and wanted to keep, but other than that I never looked at it or thought much about it for several years, but just before I turned thirty, that all changed.

CHAPTER 4

Whether it was getting ready for a garage sale or just a general house cleaning I don't remember, but the cedar chest that I stored that chronicle in had to be moved, and since it was somewhat heavy, I had to empty it out before moving it. I had left the deer skin in the same box that was given to me, and when I saw it lying in the chest, curiosity got the best of me, and I had to look inside.

A sense of wonder and fear had intrigued me when I had first received the chronicle, but over the years it had been forgotten, until now when I opened the box. All those feeling came rushing back when I saw what had happened to the seal; it wasn't golden anymore. Instead it had become nearly clear, and seemed to be filled with a white milky like substance and the lettering and markings that had been on top of the seal were gone. Its surface was now smooth to the touch, and whatever was inside swirled around every time it was moved. The diameter hadn't changed any, but it was now nearly as thin as a dime. Though the seal still seemed hard, I handled the skin carefully, not wanting to accidentally break it since it was so thin.

Slowly, I eased the skin out of the box and turned it over, but nothing had changed. Only the seal had become different, and I had no idea why. I vaguely remembered that the stranger had said something about the seal disintegrating when I turned thirty, but until now, I had dismissed it all as just a strange incident in the past. It was only a few more days until my thirtieth birthday, so I decided to leave the deer skin out of the box, and see what would happen to the seal.

Each day I would check to see what was happening to the seal, and daily it appeared to become thinner and clearer, so that the day before my birthday it was so thin and clear, that it looked like a piece of plastic wrap that had been accidentally tossed onto the skin.

Of course, as luck would have it, an emergency caused me to be out of town for several days, but the first thing I did upon returning was to check the progress of the seal. It was gone. For a moment I thought it might have become so thin that I just couldn't see it, but after feeling around where it should have been, I realized it was truly gone.

Now after all the years of wanting to see what was inside

the deer skin, you would think that I would have immediately unfolded it, but now that I could, I didn't know if I really wanted to know what was inside. I remembered what the stranger had said about something being written down in it, and that I was to translate it, but all of it seemed to be like a dream, or perhaps like something out of a science fiction book, so that now with the events actually transpiring as he said it would, that eerie feeling was back again.

Sometimes events happen in life that though we are a part of, we have no control over, and are just along for the ride, and this seemed like it was one of those times. Our actions, or lack thereof, are part of a much greater picture, but the vast majority of people will never take these things into account, and will live their lives oblivious to the fact that one individual can make a difference. It is much easier to live life in a self centered mental stupor than to be aware of all that is going on, and whether for good or bad, I was fixing to find these things out.

After several minutes of just staring at the deer skin, I decided to unfold it, and when I did I was somewhat surprised at how much writing was inside and perhaps a little bit relieved that nothing had jumped out at me or anything else out of the ordinary had happened.

The writing inside was very small and looked like someone had crammed everything together. There were no spaces between lines or letters, and it wasn't really letters I was looking at, but more of a mixture between symbols, odd lines and dots. For instance, there was what looked like a drawing of a bull, but where its front legs and head might have been, there was a diagonal line with a small dot on one side and an s shape with a circle at the end of it on the other side. The whole document seemed to be made up of these type of things, so that it really was dizzying. I found out later of course that this was the original language of all mankind, and is still the language of spiritual beings, but we are no longer physically capable of speaking it. If you can imagine it, it would be like looking at ancient Egyptian hieroglyphics, Arabic and Hebrew all mixed together, but at the same time having meaning.

Like many of the ancient languages, it read from right to left, top to bottom and no punctuation as we would relate to. The color of the ink was very strange also. It was dark when contrasted with the deer skin, but not black or brown, and it seemed to have a tint of gold color. The more you looked at it, the harder the color became to describe, and in fact it may have been one of those colors that people who have had life after death experiences, describe as being out of the normal realm of our physical abilities to see. In any event, it was definitely nothing I had ever seen before or was familiar with, but for some reason I could read it.

It was odd in that I could look at it, and have no idea what the symbols and lines meant, but could understand what it was saying when I tried reading it. It was like someone being able to translate Chinese into English, but having no idea how to read or speak Chinese. Even to this day I am baffled as to how the ability was given to me in understanding what to write down, without really understanding what was written down on the parchment.. Nevertheless, the ability to translate it was given to me, and what the reader has is that translation.

CHAPTER 5

There wasn't a lot of time to translate it all, just ninety days, but even though I knew that what was in my hands was something not only extraordinary, but one of a kind, I didn't take it as seriously as one might expect. Now where most people would have dropped all else going on in life to spend every waking hour translating it until completion, I had folded it back up and put it back in the box. Not that it wasn't on my mind, for nothing else occupied my thoughts, but I just didn't have that urgency to translate it.

This lack of urgency didn't last long though, less than a week. No more than three days after returning the document back to the box, I began to have severe headaches. They weren't migraine headaches like some people have, but seemed to have a greater intensity and would move from one point of the head to another without warning and quickly. It could be in the jaw area one moment, the eyes the next, then both at the same time. Sometimes it would be the entire facial area, but in every case it seemed as if the area was on fire, the same sensation you get when you hit your funny bone real hard, while getting hit with a hammer at the same time. That first night after these headaches started, I had a dream in which it was demanded of me to translate the document. I remembered nothing else about the dream except for that, and after another day of painful headaches and another dream, I got the message. I started translating the next day and the headaches and dreams went away.

Some days I would be so tired after work that I would only work on it for an hour or two, but usually I could get about ten hours in on the weekend. It was somewhat tedious copying a few words, reading a little more, than writing again, not to mention some of the ideas or events that were going to happen. Sometimes I had no choice but to stop and ponder some of the things I was reading. Were these things really going to happen, or was I somehow in the middle of a cosmic joke?

One of the things I noticed early on when translating the chronicle was the depth of the writing. By depth, I don't mean intellectual intensity but actual depth. There weren't any real sentences as we would think of them, but I would read a small portion, say sentence size, and after I would write it down, that sentence would be gone, and another would take its place. This would occur three times, then that particular portion of the deer skin or chronicle would become blank and I would go on to the next sentence.

At first it didn't seem like I was making any headway, but as the days then weeks went by, there was noticeable progress, and finally after filling numerous notebooks with the translation of this chronicle, I was done.

As with any large task undertaken, there was a great sense of accomplishment when it was completed, but also an emptiness. All the hours and energy spent getting it translated in the allotted time, and now it was over. No longer would I be looking at strange writing and receiving the information that had been revealed, and in a sense I felt ordinary again, and all I had to show for those weeks of work were some notebooks full of events that were going to happen in the future and a blank deerskin. I could remember what several of the symbols in the chronicle looked like, but what they meant or even the context of how they might have been used, had completely been erased from my mind.

Perhaps it was this great sense of letdown or emptiness, that led to a few months of depression, or if not depression, at least a sense that nothing in life really mattered. Also, the information contained in the chronicle, being mostly futuristic in nature, was not particularly optimistic. Not that there was a sense of doom and gloom, and not that individuals still couldn't live lives of relative happiness and ease, but that mankind had somehow allowed itself to become so enslaved to the philosophies and ideologies of a few groups of individuals, that any hope for true freedom or even the knowledge of what true freedom is had been squelched, never to take root in the mind of man again.

Also there was the rationalization that if I was to have this published, it wouldn't do any good, and even though it was written as fiction the skeptics would be out in number. All of these were factors in the chronicle not getting published in a timely manner, and as the months went by, the sense of duty or obligation I had to the stranger I had met years ago slowly faded. Not that it was a good reason, and the fact that what I had to share might have been of benefit to others never crossed my mind.

As months turned to years, I came to the realization that I would never go through the motions to get it published, and placed the notebooks in the attic where they wouldn't get lost or damaged. I did take advantage of a couple of investment opportunities that presented themselves in the book, but if I had truly followed them,

I could have made a fortune. I suppose even now one could take advantage of several opportunities, but the chronicle was not meant for that, and those who read it for that will probably end up being disappointed.

Then in the spring of 2008, I had a visit which changed everything. It was still pretty early in the evening, and I had just finished eating dinner and was sitting around watching some sporting event on the television. My wife had gone to see her parents down the street, so I was there alone. What transpired next will always be etched on my mind, and will never be taken for granted or forgotten. I forget what game I was watching, but I remember something interesting was happening when the doorbell rang, and had become a little irritated. I went and opened the door, and there was a man standing there with something in his hand, so I figured it was a salesman or something like that, but he didn't say hello or anything else, but stared at me and said

" Do you know who I am?"

Of course I didn't know who he was, but at the same instant that I started to answer, my whole body felt as if it had become engulfed in flames. I've never been in a fire, but almost everyone has burnt themselves in some way or another and this is what it felt like, only all over. The pain was indescribable it was so intense, and I wanted to scream or run or throw myself into some water, but was unable to move. It seemed like it lasted for minutes, but it suddenly stopped and I started gasping for air as if I had not been breathing during this ordeal.

"That was only five seconds," the man at the door said with a smile. It was hard to tell if it was a sinister or friendly smile, but all doubt was removed when he continued.

"Try fifteen seconds and see how it feels," he laughed.

Immediately the sensation of being on fire returned, only this time is was accompanied by a pressure that seemed like it was going to crush every bone in my body. There was no doubt in my mind that I couldn't breathe this time, and I was going to suffocate. The pain lasted for what seemed like hours and I knew that I was going to die, but just as quickly as it had started, the torture ended and nothing was physically wrong with me.

" You have just been given a taste of the torment of hell," the man at the door said, " and it was allowed for you to experience this so that you might know the seriousness of what I have to tell you."

I was terrified, and knew I was in a situation over which I had no control.

" Please don't hurt me again," I begged. " Whatever it is

you want, just let me know, but I cant go through that again." I had never really been scared of dying before now, and hadn't really given it that much thought, but after what had just transpired I was in such fear of dying, that I was literally trembling.

" Do not be afraid," the man at the door replied. " By the grace and mercy of the Creator, you will never experience an eternity of that type of torture. The choice you made many years ago sealed your escape from that destiny, but you have been given a small example of its dread, so that you will understand what I am capable of making you feel."

" Whatever I did wrong, I promise not to do it again, but please don't hurt me," I repeated.

The man reached out and touched me on the shoulder, and all the fear and dread that I had just disappeared, and was replaced by such a feeling of bliss and security, that I almost forgot the pain I had endured just moments before.

" I knew you would not recognize me, but I am T'Narg, and you have not finished the task that you were appointed for. I'm sorry that you had to go through that pain, but you have wasted nearly twenty years and my chronicle has not been published. If very many more years are allowed to pass by, its relevance and usefulness will have been compromised, and I cannot allow that to happen."

There didn't seem to be any malice in his voice, but at the same time, it didn't seem like the time to be making any excuses for not having had it published, and any reasons I had for not having done it paled in comparison to the pain I had just gone through.

" It is vitally important that you try and get it published this year," he continued. "There is no more time to waste, and frankly without this intervention, you would never have had it published, and it would sit in your attic until you died, then have been thrown away. If you were even remotely aware of the extensive preparation that went into the scribing of the chronicle, it would have never entered your mind to wait."

Remembering some of the reasons that the chronicle had been written, I asked, "Is that what you were referring to when at the beginning you said it was a testament to or maybe it was the reference to being a witness against mankind?"

T'Narg turned his head upward as if contemplating how to answer, then gave me a stare as if he were going to give me another dose of pain. The fear of the pain had subsided some, but the look he gave brought it all back again, and I could feel my knees starting to buckle. I was just about to beg for mercy again, when he answered. "No, I was talking about the seal and the preparation that goes into making one."

" What do you mean?" I queried. I guess T'Narg didn't like the tone of my voice, because he was very curt when he answered.

" All that I was commanded to reveal is in the chronicle, and nothing more is allowed to be known before the proper time. Besides that, I am here to make sure the chronicle is published, not answer questions."

" Sorry." I said. " I didn't really expect all this today, and it wasn't meant to be a sarcastic question. Its just there are so many questions I have had over the years, and now that you're here again, I thought maybe I could find out."

That seemed to appease him somewhat, and when he spoke next, it was in the kind friendly voice that I had remembered from years ago. " It was never meant for us to ever meet again, and it is your procrastination that has forced this meeting, not the need for your curiosity to be satisfied. However, I will tell you about the seal, then I must depart."

" I will only give you a brief answer, because the technology behind it will never be given to mankind nor will it be discovered before this era is over. The chronicle itself is contained within my memory, and then stored into the seal, much like you would store something onto a computer disk. Then, it goes through a preparation, so that at the proper time, which is predetermined, it becomes liquefied and forms into the words you saw on the deer skin."

This was way beyond anything I could have imagined, and I guess he could tell from the incredulous look I was giving him, that it was hard for me to find this possible. Just before I started to ask him how this could be accomplished, he continued on.

" That part of the preparing of the seal is difficult enough, but the most difficult is mind melding it into the recipient of the chronicle. As you may well remember, there have been many minor chronicles such as this one, and each and every one had to be transcribed by someone who couldn't understand what was written.

" How this mind melding is accomplished would take much to long to explain, and would be beyond your understanding, so take my word for it, that it is not only possible, but very difficult."

" But how can"

Before I could even finish the question, T'Narg interrupted and made it clear that all questions were over. " No more delay. You are to have this chronicle published as soon as possible, preferably by the end of this year. If not, I will send someone to you who will not be as nice as I was, and you will spend the remainder of your life enduring what will seem to be lifetimes of pain. I will not describe it any further than that, but you now know it is possible. Get it published."

Then, much as he did the first time we met, T'Narg turned around and walked off without a goodbye or wave or word of encouragement.

There was no doubting the seriousness and necessity of getting the chronicle published, so that very evening I pulled the notebooks out of the attic, and began typing them into manuscript form.

It took longer than I imagined it would to finish, and since I didn't know anything about the process of getting something published, that also took some time, but finally it was done, and you the reader now have it in your hands, and can determine for yourself what to make of it.

For my part the task is complete, and although I have seen and read the material many times, have seen T'Narg and felt the power of something unusual, it still seems surreal. So I tell you it is fiction, and can prove no different, and hope you benefit from the Chronicle of T'Narg.

CHAPTER 6

To those of you having the opportunity and fortune to be reading this document: greetings from the watcher T'Narg.

Throughout the history of mankind, the watchers, of whom I am one, have chronicled the events of mankind, and when necessary a chronicle of future events is given, so that those who read and understand might enlighten others and perhaps change the destiny of those they come into contact with.

Sometimes they are given to men who are to become great philosophers, others have been given to those who are to become mighty leaders, using what has been given them to better the plight of the citizens in their realm of influence, but usually they are given to ordinary men who are forgotten in the annals of history.

While all chronicles are translated and transcribed so that all to whom it was written may partake of its knowledge, most of the time only a handful of people ever see its contents, and of those who do, most of them are skeptical. And who can really blame this skepticism since future events never seem possible. After all, when it was told to those in the 1800s that man would someday travel to the moon, it was only believed by a handful of people, and they wouldn't dare make their beliefs known for fear of ridicule.

Because ordinary men are given these chronicles, and the skepticism that surrounds them, most of the chronicles vanish from the face of the earth within a decade or two, certainly within a century, and their value is lost to humanity.

But these chronicles are not given solely that mankind may benefit from its contents, but also as a testament or rather witness against the deeds they continue to do. One day each nation, as well as each individual, will have to give an accounting of not only their deeds, but of the omission of those actions which they knew were their civic and personal responsibilities to do. Perhaps at that time the importance of the chronicles will be realized, but by then it will be too late.

What a watchers duties are and who we are will be explained in much more detail momentarily, but suffice it to say for now that we are given specific areas and times to watch over and write about, and this chronicle is for the North Americans, most specifically the nation called the United States.

This particular chronicle had been given to an individual in the early 1970s and will be translated in 1988, and if all goes as planned will be published in that same year. This particular time is especially crucial, in that several key events are fixing to occur which will have dramatic social consequences.

From this time forward, all presidential elections will be predetermined by a select group of individuals whose goals are not necessarily in the best interest of the country. How this is accomplished will be detailed later, but the first attempt was with a farmer from Georgia, and because his winning seemed unrealistic considering his qualifications, it was a complete disaster when he did win.

More insight into this fiasco will come later, but it was such a failure that there was little chance that another candidate of his ilk could be elected, and as expected the people chose a man who not only had moral fortitude and courage, but he also had the country's best interest at heart. This president will serve diligently for two terms, but after that all future presidents will be chosen for the people by outsiders. The next president will even talk about the need for the existence of a new world order, but very few will really realize what he is saying, and the dangers associated with it.

Another great happening is going to be the explosion of personal computers. Until now the complex learning curve has kept ordinary people from learning how to use computers, but soon it will become extremely easy to use, and the speed of communication along with a multitude of available functions will make it a household appliance almost as popular as television. The ease with which people will be able to communicate with one another, even those of other countries, will lead to the change of several social structures.

Educational philosophies are beginning to change, as well as economics, and what have been social norms for centuries will be challenged in the arena of ideas.

Mankind is also in the beginning of what will become one of the greatest viral epidemics of all history. Because much of the details and knowledge of this virus is in its beginning stages, many false assumptions have been made, and this will be further explained also.

There are other events and ideas which are soon going to come to the forefront, but this is the beginning of an era which if mankind is to survive, it must be understood how and why these events are occurring, and perhaps change the outcome.

These events have such momentum, that it is very unlikely

that anyone can stop it, but if enough people realize what is happening and do try to stop it, then possibly it might be slowed and eventually even reversed.

Why these events are happening, who is behind it, and how it is being propagated on man will be explored, but first, a brief explanation of what the role and purpose of a watcher is. By better understanding who we are and what our primary function is, the reader will begin to be more aware of how we can write our chronicles authoritatively, and that it is in their best interest to heed its contents.

CHAPTER 7

Watchers, as the name implies, have been watching over the affairs of mankind ever since they were created to dwell on the earth. More importantly, we chronicle the events so that they are not lost to history, and if it becomes necessary this chronicle can also be used as a witness against men's actions.

We do not chronicle the acts of specific individuals, but rather the actions of nations and cities, and groups which can and sometimes do have great influences over the destinies of these nations. For instance, the activities of all political parties are chronicled, but so are those of such organizations like organized crime and churches. Any group which has an influence on the nation, city or any other body of people, will be taken into account.

It is not only their actions that we chronicle, but also the underlying philosophy which drives the group to exist and have its being. Motive for existence can be as reliable a witness as actions. Many groups have their foundation and purpose in being opposed to another group, and in instances where hatred and violence are concerned, it makes little difference whether any deeds are actually carried out or not.

Even though intent can be a witness, something needs to be clarified before continuing. Watchers are not given the responsibility of judging intentions, and mankind is incapable of it. Just because someone belongs to a organization which harbors those individuals that have racist agendas, of whatever color, it does not automatically make them guilty by association, but be warned. Those who do find their friendships and community values within these associations, will be looked upon unfavorably. What excuse can be given for condoning another's behavior by your presence? However, know that there is One who can judge your intention, and it is for that One that we write our chronicles. Watchers do however have the ability in certain severe cases to decide or decree what punishment may befall a group or individual, but the actual sentence and judgment of guilt is not ours to make.

As stated before, we do not chronicle the activities of individuals, except in those extremely rare cases where the individual is so charismatic or has so much power, that they are a group or force unto themselves.

Nebuchadnezzar who was king of Babylon nearly 3000 years ago was such an individual. He had become so powerful and wealthy, that he had become like a god, not only to himself, but to the people of the world. It came to be such a problem, that it was necessary to intervene, and this was one of those times that the watchers decreed what should happen. Even in this case we did not pass sentence, but only decreed what the sentence should be.

All the watchers agreed that if left unchecked, people would soon forget that there is One who places men in power, and He gives it to whom he wills, and can take it away as well. The sentence was agreed upon, and Nebuchadnezzar was removed from power that very hour, until his power and pride had been humbled.

Another example of a decree being given by the watchers, this time against a city, occurred much earlier in the history of mankind, and many are familiar with its story. Two cities, and several small villages, had become so debased and perverted in their behavior towards one another, that even the watchers were becoming too disgusted to look upon and chronicle the events. The perversion had reached such a level, that intervention would be pointless, and it was decreed that the cities and all things within them, living or not, were to be destroyed, cleansed by the searing flame of fire.

The sentence was so severe and final, that the One came down Himself to see if these things were so. It wasn't as if the One was unaware of what was happening, but so that it would be chronicled that the One was sympathetic towards man and righteous in passing such a sentence. The perversion was greater than we had dared write about, and the sentence was passed, and the cities were destroyed, never to be inhabited by man or beast again. These events are written in greater detail and can be found in the Great Chronicle, for those wishing for more information.

Watchers write numerous chronicles, most of which are stored in archives, but of the ones given to mankind which tell of future events, nearly all disappear within two or three decades, as was mentioned before. However, the one that we call the Great Chronicle, cannot be destroyed, and will exist until the end of the ages.

This particular chronicle was written by the One, whom we also call the Creator, and was given to mankind, so that all people in all nations might know what that early period of humanity was like, where they came from, where they are going, and what their duty and purpose on earth is. Past, present and future all combined in one chronicle, and that as created beings, what our responsibility to the Creator consists of.

Because of the importance of this Great Chronicle, there have been those who have tried to have it eradicated from the face of the earth, but all attempts fail. Not only do all attempts fail, but this chronicle is in more homes of the world than any other book. Yet for all the wide spread distribution the Great Chronicle has, it is only read and studied by a minute fraction of those who have it in their possession. We watchers have always been puzzled by this phenomenon. How can such an important document written by the One, the Creator, be in the hands of so many, yet the desire to know what secrets and history and information it might contain, is just not there.

Over the ages, watchers see many great things happen, as well as many terrible things, but this is perhaps one of the saddest. On that day of accountability, there will be many who say they didn't know this or didn't know that, but when they find out that the information was available for them to know, and was in their possession, their mouths will be silent. We mourn over this dilemma and do what we can, but where is that wise one who will listen?

Nearly all watchers dwell here upon the earth, and have been here since the beginning, or soon thereafter. At first, few watchers were needed, since there weren't many inhabitants of the earth yet, but as populations grew and man spread throughout the earth, more watchers were sent to keep track and chronicle events.

I, T'Narg, have been here for 6,834 years. You might wonder how long I have existed, or how old I am, but time belongs to the physical world, and we are spiritual beings. In the spiritual realm, there is no time, only eternity, and it was only when we entered the physical realm that we understood or rather were subjected to the concept of time. We do not age, and since we rarely see anyone more than once, we always appear in a form which would be the least alarming to that particular individual.

It is not necessary for our survival that we have things like food, water and shelter, even air is not a necessity, but we do enjoy these things. Physical beings must have these things to survive, and if the partaking of these necessities also brings joy, that is an added benefit, but for us it is a delight. Something as simple as drinking a glass of water can be euphoric, and words cannot truly describe it. To know that something was created by the One, and that wherever it came from, whether artic regions, a river, lake, etc, and no matter how long it may have existed, its whole purpose in being, or existing, was so that you might drink it at a particular time in history; that is humbling, and that is what we taste. Because of this great delight we can have in partaking of the physical things of this world, many of the watchers as well as many angels fell into disgrace early in human history.

Watchers and angels were created at the same time, and except for our duties, there is relatively little difference. Because our duties are somewhat limited when compared to the angels, it was not necessary to have large numbers of watchers, and after the rebellion, we were practically decimated.

Not only now, but throughout the chronicle, there are times when a brief history of how certain social establishments came into being will greatly enhance the understanding of the reader. Many of the events that will be foretold later in the chronicle, will need to have that historical foundation in order that the symbiotic relationships of the events can be more easily seen.

We are not permitted to divulge the full details of the rebellion, but it was initially started by a group of angels, and it was their deception, along with the lust for human wives, that many of the watchers were persuaded into joining the rebellion. While the result of the ungodly unions between the watchers and human women cannot be discussed here, it is briefly mentioned in the Great Chronicle, and insinuates why we are few in number, and likened as the angels.

The watchers and angels who remained with the One, were not only appalled by what we saw, but were astonished at the punishment meted out by the One. We were so fearful that in the eons to come it might be possible for another rebellion to occur, that we begged the Creator to have mercy, and make us incapable of such treachery. Assurances were given to us that there would be no more rebellions, and in fact the current one had not ended but would be played out over many thousands of years.

Originally the rebellion had been instigated by the one angel who was created greater than all the others. His wisdom, beauty and power so exceeded the other beings of the Ones creation, that this angel became prideful and started demanding worship which is solely reserved for the One. This rebellion was somewhat overlooked in its early stages, but as it gained momentum, it became necessary for the Creator to step in and squelch it.

Some were bound with irremovable chains and thrown into dungeons of darkness, while the rest were banished to the realm of the earth. This was to be a temporary punishment, and their ultimate and final destiny is described in more detail in the Great Chronicle.

Knowing their final end greatly incensed these rebellious

ones, and as their corruption grew, so did their hatred of the One. This hatred grew to such a level, that they decided they would ruin the Creators greatest accomplishment; man.

Books could be and have been written about the rebellion, but it is not the intent of this chronicle to talk of history, but of events to take place around the time of the lives of the reader, so no more will be said, except that it is the rebellion that has created the situation man is in today.

CHAPTER 8

The primary focus of this chronicle is the United States, for the events fixing to take place are in large part due to its being a superpower in the world. The status of being a world power, and at the same time having founding principles which gives individual rights to the citizenry, make it a prime target for those wishing to have world dominance over all peoples.

Its unique founding was based on the fact that it is the Creator who determines how governments and people are to interact, and laws and principles of government function should reflect that. People were not to be tools of government, but government was to make sure those rights given by the Creator were not inhibited by any source, whether from within or without. However, the government was also not to be a tool of those people who would use it for their own personal gain.

Those leaders who formed your bill of rights and constitution, were men who had studied the Great Chronicle, and understood the evil and depravity of the heart of man, and placed safeguards within that constitution. This was done by splitting the federal government into three branches, each having specific duties, and the ability to circumvent another branch if it overstepped its authority. The individual states within this federal government were given the most power, and it was understood that the federal government had no jurisdiction or right to interfere in the affairs of these states. Its primary function was to make sure that no state passed laws contrary to the principles set forth in the constitution, and to provide a common defense against attack.

In the past, it would not have been necessary to mention the basic principle that were behind the founding of this country, for it was taught in your educational institutions, but now it is purposefully omitted for reasons which will be clearer later. Even now, some of the readers of this chronicle will understand, but as stated earlier, there must be some history mentioned, so that the reader might have a better understanding of the situation. It will be an incomplete history of course, but the wise reader will search further.

These men who founded your country were so convinced that those freedoms given by the Creator were not to be infringed on by any government, that good men, educated men, must be willing to give up their lives for the freedom of all. And many of them did die, or spent all their resources in the pursuit of this republic called the United States.

It took a great war with a power much mightier than them, but eventually they won, and the republic which resulted was the greatest experiment of self government in the history of the world. Because the principles of self government were ones found in the Creators Great Chronicle, the growth and power of this great country grew quickly, and it was apparent to all, friend and foe alike, that it was a country which the One kept a providential eye on and blessed. This infuriated those who had designs for a united world, and their efforts will be explained shortly, but a foundation must be set before anything will make sense to the reader.

This country was not perfect by any means, but it had been set up in such a way that any time flaws became apparent, it could be dealt with swiftly so that the good of all men might be upheld.

Slavery was a prime example of a flaw that was allowed to continue much to long, and no government that wished to call itself one watched over by the Creator could allow it to continue. True godly men, as they sometimes called themselves, could not allow any member of the human race to be considered property, or to be enslaved by others, so the practice was abolished.

Evil does not go quietly away, and slavery was resisted by war, but eventually the practice was discontinued. However, those groups which have always wished to enslave men remained, and the agricultural and business trades they had established were still strong and thrived.

The great institution of slavery still exits in different forms today, though it isn't seen as men owning other men, but enslaving them in other ways which will be seen more clearly later. As reprehensible as slavery is, sometimes being a slave and not knowing it is worse than being a slave in the technical sense. There are those who enslave others, such as drug dealers who enslave their clients, that are in much greater bondage to an immorality which will one day be their greatest regret.

Those of us (watchers), who saw our fellow watchers fall in the rebellion, know what it is like to see those we care about fall into a slavery, a spiritual slavery if you will, and we mourn for mankind as we see the increased slavery it is falling under. It is another reason we write chronicles, so that some might heed them and try and change the course of not only their lives, but of those around them.

Despite the flaws which flared up from time to time, this great experiment called the United States succeeded and became a shining light in a dark world. Ideals such as equality, justice and liberty were so engrained in the hearts of the citizens, that those from all over the world came to be a part of this great experiment and to free themselves from the tyranny of those governments which still thought liberty was just an idea to be crushed.

No one imagined that in less than two hundred years, this country would grow to become a world super power, and now is the only superpower. In just a little over a year, you will see the fall of the Soviet Union, another failed attempt at government trying to control every aspect of peoples lives. There are other countries now that are strong, and several which are going to equal the United States in economic and military power, but only because many of the principles which made you great, are going to be diluted.

Unfortunately the same principles which made it such a success, are the same ones which are hated by those opposed to the One. The tendency for other countries to be jealous of the successes of another also contribute to the friction which is just now starting to rear its ugly head. As with people, countries see what another has, and starts scheming on how to take it from them.

In reality however, it is several groups which have been trying to dominate all peoples and governments, which are the real problem. Some of these groups have existed hundreds of years, some mere decades, but they all tend to have a common denominator, and a common goal.

We see each generation of mankind make the same type of mistakes over and over again, and it distresses us to see such ignorance. The old adage that the only thing man learns from history is that man learns nothing from history is very true, but it will soon be seen why that is not altogether by accident.

CHAPTER 9

Education is one of the main tools used to keep the mass of people ignorant, and this is particularly noticeable when we come to the subject of history. This makes it somewhat difficult for a watcher, in that it is necessary to make sure the reader of a chronicle understands that past events usually have a bearing on future events. Then when events or trends fixing to take place are revealed, they make much more sense.

For example, in the next twenty years, the presidency of the United States will be in the hands of two families. A father and his son will hold the position for twelve years, with another individual in between the two holding it for eight. Even though it will appear that the three are very different in their policies, upon closer examination it will be found that they have moved in a very similar direction.

Much more will be explained about the role politics plays in this chronicle, but for now, this is just an example of how easy it is to make a statement, but explaining why this is so, is quite different.

To the uneducated mind, and by uneducated I do not mean unintelligent, the personalities and actions of these three presidents make it quite difficult to discern their common goals. However, when we look at the organizations they are members of, the goals of these organizations, and how they were groomed for this position, it becomes apparently clear that the three of them are quite similar.

The impact these groups have worldwide cannot be overemphasized, and the reader usually must be reeducated in order that they can understand the techniques used to control not only the outcome of circumstances, but the publics perception of these circumstances.

In past centuries it would have been quite easy to just describe the few groups which existed then , and then concentrate on techniques, but these techniques have been perfected to such a degree and so infiltrated your society, that the presence of these groups are generally not noticed.

From time to time, someone will come along who

understands what is going on, but the moment they try and go public with the information, they are labeled either as eccentric, or a conspiracy theory nut.

There have always been conspiracy theories, and even in 1988 there will be many, but as personal computers gain popularity, the ability to communicate these theories will grow, as will the number of conspiracies. Not only that, but over the last one hundred years, these several groups have evolved into many smaller ones which specialize in one particular area or another, making it difficult to understand their symbiotic relationship.

Later, when these organizations are examined further, it will become apparent that it is actually only a few individuals who control all of them, and then perhaps the reader of the chronicle will begin to understand the large degree to which many of the events are purposefully orchestrated.

Most of the time the events and even the people involved might seem random, but when one sees all the pieces, the harmony with which it all fits is uncanny. To give a brief example, I will explain a little about the oil wars which are going to occur in the 21st century. A much fuller description will come later, but this is just to show how random events actually have been coordinated to fulfill a desired result.

In the early 1990s, a militant Islamic terrorist group will bomb the twin towers in New York City, and in following years will commit several apparently random attacks against the United States in several different places around the world. Though some attention will be given to these attacks, to a large extent they will be ignored, until an event in the early 21st century which will awaken people out of their stupor.

This will be called in the decades to come, the actual beginning of the oil wars. For the individuals who perpetrated this act, it had religious overtones, but for those who actually planned and created the opportunity, it was one of financial and political. It actually helped further the ultimate end of those who are the puppet masters, in that it helped in further unifying countries against a supposed common enemy.

The depths to which these groups will go to fulfill their ultimate goal is something which the reader is now beginning to grasp, so I will concentrate on how, or rather what techniques are being used to ensnare mankind. It is only then that we can describe the ones who are perpetrating this on humanity.

Something to keep in mind when reading about these techniques, is that they are not a end in themselves, but tools to be used in shaping societies and minds into the intended goal. One must constantly be on guard though, for most of the time the idea or technique is presented as an end in itself, when it is actually only a part of the picture. As we shall see in a moment, education is a perfect example of this.

No matter what time period or country a watcher might chronicle in the history of mankind, there are three major techniques used to infiltrate and influence society, and these are finance, education and propaganda. Politics or government, religion, and of course violence, whether through organized crime or war, have roles to play, but it is more in the realm of making sure the first three techniques are implemented, than in their own right as tools, and it is vital that the reader understands this. The role government and religion plays, especially in the next twenty or thirty years, will greatly influence not only the way finance and education is viewed by the general public, but the way propaganda is used will also be a major factor in shaping public opinion. .

When one first looks at finance, it seems to have a minor role to play in the scheme of things, but upon closer examination, you will begin to understand that it is the greatest tool or weapon these organizations have, and it is largely through education and propaganda that its significance has been downplayed.

Finance can also be one of the trickiest tools to use, as

many times a positive benefit in one area creates a negative in another, so its use must be orchestrated with the finest of care. Its greatest use though, is to enslave, and this can be done in various ways, all of them effective, and will be expanded on later.

The necessity of a chronicle is generally in order that future events will be unfolded to those desiring to be enlightened, so that enough people might be energized to bring about a positive change for the future of mankind, and that wisdom might be imparted while doing so. As I, T'Narg, illuminate the future through the techniques being used, let it be known that throughout the centuries I have seen these tools used with great effectiveness, and there is little hope that a paradigm shift in the thinking of mankind will occur, but perhaps…

CHAPTER 10

The role of education is like a two edged sword. On the one hand, it is very necessary if society is to progress, but in the wrong hands, it can be used to mold the minds of individuals into whatever purpose best serves the wielder, not the student.

A thorough knowledge of the history of education would greatly benefit the reader, but for the purposes of this chronicle, just a few highlights will be explored.

In times past, a formal education was reserved solely for those of royalty or for those whose economic means might acquire it for their posterity, but for the general public, it was either forbidden, or not within their financial grasp.

It was always understood that the more education one had,

the greater chances of a prosperous life, or at least a financially prosperous life, but at a certain point in time, it was realized that if it was possible to take children from their parents in the guise of educating them, then the children's minds could be molded.

Throughout the centuries, public education has been tried in several countries, but now in the 1980s, nearly 90s, almost every country in the world has some form of public education. In the past, most of these have been modeled after the United States, but increasingly, especially after the turn of the century, other countries will have more of a practical application for education, while the U.S. and other western nations will adopt more of a social awareness type of education.

For the most part logic based education had always been taught, the staples being mathematics, the various sciences, and literature, which included the skills of writing and reading and the learning of different languages. As each level within these arts required knowledge derived from a previous level, a student had to think, and come to conclusions based on past learning. This in turn caused one to think of all problems or events in life in a logical manner, so that when events of whatever manner occurred, the student could see the conclusion or the perceived conclusion of an event, based on past probabilities.

Compulsory public education was relatively unheard of until the middle of the 19th century, but its usefulness in molding minds, and in bridging the gap between the wealthy and poor, quickly became apparent. Great strides were being made in all sectors, whether business or societal needs, but great unrest was brewing also, as the masses became educated as to the way they had been treated as property.

Men who understood what this unrest would lead to, decided the philosophy of education had to change, so between 1910 and 1920 the purposeful and methodical dumbing down of the American public school system began.

Knowing it would take several decades before a noticeable decline in such areas as mathematics and language skills would be able to be capitalized on, it was decided that a strong emphasis on patriotism would and could have the desired effect of creating individuals whose sole allegiance was to the state. This patriotism emphasized the supremacy of the state, rather than an adherence to founding ideologies, and it would be just a matter of time before personal rights could to be taken away under the disguise of patriotism.

These rights, many of them guaranteed by the constitution, will be removed either by the will of the people through democratic processes, or by illegitimate and or immoral judges. Judicial activism, as it will be called, will be especially prevalent early in the next century, and by 2015 most rights as you recognize them now, will be gone.

Idiocy will rule in the minds of many of these judges, as they will use arguments such as evolving constitutions, to change established institutions, but unfortunately by time this occurs, most citizens will have been indoctrinated by public education to believe what has been told them. This environment will be perfect for business and government alike, for they have always worked hand in hand, and with an educational system in place which created citizens who could not think for themselves, or question authority, a new type of slavery had begun.

The patriotism and socialization of the individual seemed to have an almost immediate effect, so much so, that when the newly formed United Nations began making up different declarations of humans rights, it was decided that compulsory public education was a right for all citizens of the world.

This United Nations is the vehicle that these organizations I have mentioned will use to eventually control the world. It will be the ultimate in government; a one world government with all nations under its authority. Right now it doesn't seem to have great authority, but by 2000 it will have greatly increased its power, and will have all its laws it wishes to impose on the world in place.

Several attempts will have been made to tax the nations and its citizens, so it can have funds for a military solely funded and under U.N. command, but it will not be until late in the 2010s that this will be accomplished.

Even now, it is the United States that is the greatest obstacle in this governing body being able to take control. That is why the re-education of your citizenry needs to take place, in order that it be a smooth transition from nation to a nation state. All the other major nations have had their citizens beholden to the state through various government programs for so long, that to question authority isn't even an option. That doesn't mean that there isn't dissention from time to time, but it is so insignificant, that it really doesn't exist.

The individualism which helped make the U.S. such a strong country, is also a hindrance in the plans of the United Nations, so educational programs will increasingly give way to philosophies where the group consensus prevails over individualism. Business leaders and government officials alike were elated that finally there would be an apparatus in place which could train and educate workers without giving them the skills necessary to question the social and political order. What is so unfortunate about this predicament, is that for the most part, everyone will be satisfied with the status quo, and as long as nothing affects them personally, it either must not matter, or isn't important. The great tide of apathy will have come to shore.

Not only will most individuals not be able to process the affairs going on around them, but there will be a increasing inability to communicate in a meaningful manner. The explosion of personal computers, and the mass use of cell phones which will occur in the beginning of the 21st century, will make the necessity of written communication almost obsolete.

The great shift to social education over individualism began with earnest in the 1970s, and while to some degree, individual achievement is still recognized, it has all but disappeared. By the turn of the century, nearly all learning activities will be group orientated. Group participation in subjects such as mathematics will be normal, and by 2010 it will be considered an oddity if anyone tries to solve problems on their own.

When group participation was first introduced, it was met with some skepticism, for the more intelligent and motivated students were consistently doing all the work, with the group as a whole getting credit, but as time goes on, you will notice that this anomaly will work itself out, in fact the result will be desired. The rising resentment of the gifted students, those doing most of the academic work, will eventually create an atmosphere where no one is willing to strive for academic excellence, and these gifted students will either leave the system by dropping out of school, or refuse to cooperate with the group.

This will give rise to further declines in academic achievement, and by 2010, those students graduating from high school, and even college, will not have much more education than a sixth grader of the early 1900s. Individualism will have virtually ceased to exist, and any form of self achievement will be frowned upon.

There will be resistance to this type of education, and this will be the cause of the great explosion in home schooling you are just now beginning to see. Declining academic standards will not be the only reason for home schooling, but the increase in school violence, teaching of immoral philosophies and the secularization of education, will be major factors. Also, an increasing hatred of religious convictions, especially Christianity, will cause many parents to opt out of the government run schools.

There have always been some students that were home schooled, and they were always looked upon as a novelty, as they are now, but as the numbers increase, so will the resistance by the government agencies affected by this phenomenon.

Right now the number of home schooled children is relatively small, in the thousands, but by 2000, there will be nearly a million, and by 2010 when it peaks, several million will be in the ranks of the home schooled. While the resistance to home schooling is very small now, each student not enrolled in government schools represents a financial loss to the increasingly cumbersome school administrations, and the unwillingness of these administrations to downsize will create tension between parents and the government.

At first, some school districts and states declared that home schooling was illegal, but without any clear laws in place, this tactic failed, so they tried to control curriculums. This tactic also failed, as students taught in home schools generally scored much higher in the governments own standardized tests, using much different curriculums than that of the public institutions.

Realizing the danger that a large educated group of citizens would be to globalization, many states started using their child welfare agencies as weapons to intimidate parents. Illegally entering into homes and interrogating children will become common practice early in the next century, and in many cases the children will be snatched from the parents. Not only will they be taken away, but many times the interrogations will be as intense as criminal ones. Very little will be known about this, as the media, a major propaganda tool for the government, will not publicize this, except in those rare cases where abuse may be happening.

Most other nations have had their educational programs under control for several decades, and in the case of third world countries it is virtually non existent, so this will be increasingly embarrassing for the United States. Brazil and Germany had made home schooling illegal when compulsory education was first introduced, and since they had no problems controlling the educational system in their countries, it will be declared illegal by the United Nations to continue home schooling.

This edict by the United Nations will be met with resistance and court battles, but it will only take seven years, from 2015 to 2022, to completely eradicate it from the U.S. With all the negative media attention against those who do home school, this eradication will be welcomed by the general public, and in less than a generation, most will never remember that it even existed.

While re-education is going to be very necessary, propaganda, or media as it is more commonly referred to, will need to be in the hands of a very few individuals, while at the same making the appearance of being a free press.

CHAPTER 11

What is freedom of the press? At one point of time, it meant that government could not curtail the dispensation of ideas, opinions and events, or even embarrassing information; there was to be no restraint. This did not mean that untruths could be published, or that malicious lies and rumors designed to defame could be published, but beyond that, it was necessary for the citizens of a free nation to be informed.

It was considered so essential to the continuance of a free society, that it was included in the first amendment of your constitution. It was also included in the Universal Declaration of Human Rights where the United Nations, which was briefly mentioned before, determined it was an essential right to have expression of ideas and opinions, and to use whatever means of media that was available.

Ironically, many member nations, most notably those with

dictatorships or non democratic governments, agreed these were basic human rights, but in practice refused this access to their citizens. In some ways this appeared to be problematic, but since most of the rights guaranteed by the United Nations were being broken by all nations, it was generally seen as a minor infraction, and overlooked.

Knowing a free press prohibited wide scale propaganda from being effective, the concerted effort by a small group of individuals to own media outlets, whether radio, television, or print, began in earnest. Newspapers posed little problems, for they had for the most part been monopolized for years, and radio, except for those days before television, was ineffective.

However, television proved to be more difficult to control. Not that gaining ownership was a problem, for from the very outset it was in the hands of like minded individuals, but making it appear as if each station had something unique to offer the viewer was a different matter.

With only three stations to really choose from, viewers expected, even demanded a variety of programming, and wanted to be entertained, not philosophized or preached to. While nightly news was generally choreographed by these stations in order that no conflicting points of view might accidentally be presented to the public, entertainment programming was generally varied.

But now, with the great growth and popularity of satellite and cable television, not only can one view programming 24 hours a day, but the variety is as numerous as there are interests. Even though there is an enormous amount of programming available now, by the turn of the century there will be so many channels, that there will be channels solely devoted as guides for upcoming shows.

However, even with this great proliferation and growth of television, ownership will remain in the hands of a relatively small group, which will make their efforts to distract the masses, that much easier.

The advent of television will turn out to be the greatest marketing and propaganda tool in all the history of mankind. Though it will be rivaled in a few years by the personal computer with what will be called the world wide web, or internet, it will still be television that dominates the media.

One of the main, if not the main reason that television is the dominate tool of propaganda, is its propensity to be addictive. Those who control all this media were quite aware from the very start that this would probably happen, as they were also intimately involved with its early development.

Whenever an individual views television, their brain changes the way it normally thinks, and it becomes passive, and very highly suggestible. It is very similar to being hypnotized, and makes any suggestion, whether positive or negative, seem plausible, and it becomes the viewers own idea, though they have no recollection where this idea came from.

This does not need to be done subliminally, though it is sometimes used, but an inferior education which created the inability to discern and dissect ideas, made the television a perfect way to sway the opinion of viewers at will. Most of the time it will be very illogical, but to an untrained mind, it makes perfect sense. It will go something like this.

From time to time, someone acclaimed for moral standing, usually a preacher, will have some moral failing, many times in the area he or she is most outspoken against. So the argument will be that since he spoke out against this behavior, but was involved in it, anyone else who speaks out against it is probably involved in it also. When the next person does speak out, they will very likely be slandered, and at the very least have their character attacked, as unworthy to speak on this matter, as they are most likely involved in the behavior also. As can be seen, there is no logic to this, but these kinds of attacks, and this type of propaganda, will be used relentlessly in television programs, sometimes subtly, sometimes not.

Another way in which television creates addiction, is that in many people chemicals are produced by the body while watching, that stimulates the pleasure mood. This creates not only a situation where someone wants to watch more, to feel better, but it creates physical idleness as well. This will grow into such a problem, that by 2010, most of your population will be considered overweight and in poor health.

By this time, the difference between reality and fantasy will have become so blurred, that most people will not have any opinions of their own, but will parrot those heard uttered by their favorite actor, or newscaster. These mush minds will no longer be capable of forming intelligent thought out opinions, and will have virtually become enslaved. Later, when the role of finance is explained, you will see how heavy the chains of enslavement have already become, and by 2000 it will be much worse.

As fewer and fewer people become unable to distinguish between the reality of life and the fantasy of television, this group who controls the media, or the Society as I will refer to them, will begin using actors as spokesmen to spread their doctrines. It will not matter, or even occur to the listener, that their favorite actor or actress is just a voice, and usually has no expertise in the topic they are talking about. Most of the time, the act will be so convincing, that one can only assume that the speaker believes or has been led to believe, that everything they say is truthful and important. It will not really matter though, as the mush minded disciples who listen to their favorite idol, will hang onto their every word, and treat it as gospel.

This will be particularly effective when it comes to spreading panic among the public. Many of the organizations, and the ideologies they espouse, will be nothing more than veiled attempts to create dissension among the citizenry, and to gain further control over their lives. This is nothing new of course, as groups like these have always been around, but the propaganda of television will give them a greater voice and more credibility. How else could groups with such racist beginnings as Planned Parenthood, get government funding for an ideology which is little more than population control and eugenics. In twelve years there will be what is called the Y2K scare, which will be nothing more than a panic attack, but it will keep peoples minds off more important matters.

Anything and everything will be fair game in the attempt to create a constant state of anxiety. From the farce that will be known as man made global warming, to asteroids nearly hitting earth, to the threat of biological disasters, whether real or imagined, each threat will be just another attempt to make individuals more dependent on government rather than themselves.

Using actors to create a sense of unrest in the mush minds is effective, but the real usefulness of these idols can be seen in the way they can influence political elections, particularly presidential ones. Though the role politics plays in the plans of The Society will be further unveiled later, a quick example will be given of how this will work in the presidential election just twelve years from now. Maybe now the reader will begin to understand that free elections are a thing of the past.

The governor of Texas will be running against the vice president, a man many will consider to be intellectually bankrupt , (which they will appear to have proof of in just a few short years), and the numbers will be so skewed in favor of the governor from Texas, that it will be necessary for The Society to intervene on behalf of the vice president.

This intervention was so effective in not only creating a close race, but in creating tension, even hatred, among several different groups, a strategy which works perfectly for future plans of The Society. The race will be so close that the losers will claim that they were defrauded out of the presidency, and the fallout between your two political parties will be felt for several decades to come.

Actors will be so enraged that the candidate they had been convinced to support lost, that just eight years later, they will throw all their efforts behind another unqualified individual in an effort to redeem themselves, not to the public, but to themselves. Of course, this will play right into the hands of The Society, for both candidates will have global agendas, although the one backed by the actors makes no pretense of it.

Though this is just a sampling of how the idols will be used to propagate public opinion, many other incidents could be mentioned and many more will occur, but these are just mentioned in order to show the sway and effectiveness these actors have.

While there are many television addicts even now, as the quality of the TV sets becomes better, and the proliferation of available channels goes up, so will the addictions. By 2010, there will be so many different channels, that virtually everyone will have something of interest to watch. Everything imaginable will be covered, even channels devoted to weather will be popular. Amusements, hobbies, drama, finance, news, it will all be at the fingertips of the audience.

Sport aficionados will be elated at the vast number of different sports that are being televised, so much so, that these channels will generally outdo any other genre of programming. It actually will turn into an ironic situation, for it had been relatively easy to draw women into the fantasy world of soap operas, but the world of sports will draw in much larger numbers of men.

Calling sports a fantasy world seems contradictory, when it is an actual event taking place in real time, and it perhaps could be said with more clarity, that it is a distraction, but it is exactly this distraction from life, that makes it a fantasy world.

In fact, this will spawn a whole new industry, known as fantasy role playing. Devotees will be able to have their own teams, in a variety of different sports, competing against other players with their own teams. It will grow quickly, leagues with commissioners will form, and even professional athletes on whom these teams are based, will play in these fantasy games.

These great distractions from life and reality, will keep large sections of the population in a mental stupor, unaware that anything is wrong. Several decades from now, sociologists will study and write about this phenomenon, but by then there will be to few people who notice or care.

Infused with these distractions, will be the gradual moral

decay of society. Shows will increasingly depict immoral behavior as normal, so often, that this behavior will start to become socially acceptable. Approximately every ten years, some type of immoral behavior or language is inserted into programming, in order to diminish normal standards of morality. This will be met with opposition for a few weeks, but as the shows continue on, and people get used to the change, the opposition disappears. In the next thirty years, unbelievable immoral behaviors will become such common place, that unless one saw it, it would not be believed.

The propaganda techniques used to change beliefs are almost always the same, and quite effective. Most of the time, those portraying immoral lifestyles, are made to look intelligent, friendly, loving and caring for the well being of their fellow human beings, while those in opposition are either violent, crazy, stupid and unattractive, or a combination of all these characteristics. By using these tactics, and injecting complete falsehoods into the dialogue, the mush minds who view this come to the erroneous conclusion that not only is the behavior acceptable, but those who disagree, have no right to that opinion.

It wont take long, and by 2020, any type of programming will be allowed, no matter how violent, vile or pornographic. The

Society does not particularly care about those who are adulterers, sodomites, murderers, thieves, and abusers of the innocent, in fact they loathe them, but they are useful in the destruction of morality in society. When there are no morals, might makes right, and when you control the might and the citizenry have become lost in a world of fantasy, then humanity is essentially chained. The importance immorality has, though negatively, will be more clearly seen, when the future of religion is revealed, for it is the true religion of the Creator that the Society fights against.

Before the role that radio will have in the future is explored, there is one more interesting part that television will play in the future. Twenty one years from now, in 2009, all televisions will receive their programming digitally, either through cable or satellite. No longer will analog be used.

By then, a large percentage of households will be receiving digitally anyway, so it will not seem unusual that this is happening, but the real reason behind it, is somewhat sinister. It will seem far fetched and impractical to the reader of today, but by then, it will seem plausible, almost welcome. Of course, the main reason for doing this is economical, or at least that is what the public will be told, but the secondary reason is for increased surveillance of the citizenry.

There have always been those misinformed individuals who are convinced that televisions is spying on them, sending pictures and information about them to some secret government database, but by 2009, the actual technology to accomplish this will be available. Many of the personal computers by then will have miniature cameras installed in them in order that people can see one another as they communicate, either on the phone or by what will be called e-mail. It will be perfectly normal, and unobtrusive.

Several unauthorized government experiments will be done in 2005, in order to see how effective it would be in monitoring the activities of ordinary citizens, and if it could be useful in curtailing illegal activities. The experiments proved very effective, even preventing several attacks by those planning terrorist attacks (this is the term that will be used to describe the attacks of the enemy during the start of the oil wars), and it was decided that this was the future of national security.

Between 2010 and 2015, there will be further studies, this time with willing participants, in order to work out any possible quirks in the systems. The greatest difference between these studies, and the previous ones, will be in that not only will the participants be seen and heard, but it will be possible for the monitors to speak directly to them as well as be seen. Participants will not be able to contact the monitors directly, but monitors can at anytime speak to participants.

During these five years, the technology will be perfected, but it will be 2020 before the public will be persuaded to accept it inside their televisions. Activation will be on a complete voluntary basis, sometimes with compensation, but in 2025 it will be mandated that all televisions be activated. This will be done in the guise of public safety, and national security, but it will really only be used to monitor the activities of those dissenters who try and persuade others of the control government has on them.

CHAPTER 12

With the inception of television, newspapers and radio quickly found themselves dwindling in importance. They will always be around, as newspapers are necessary to disperse the information a newscast or entertainment program just cant do in its allotted time, and radio has such a variety of music, local and national sports, and other programming, that it would be virtually impossible to do without these two media outlets.

However, at virtually the same time this chronicle is revealed in 1988, an interesting phenomenon will occur in radio. There have always been talk radio shows, but generally they have been religious in nature, and market share has always been relatively low. But this year, an individual claiming he has "talent on loan from God", or the Creator as we watchers would say, will begin a talk show that will explode onto the scene, and will in years to come, be known as the beginning of conservative talk radio.

It will be a few years before the name, conservative talk show, actually catches on, because more than anything, it is just common sense. Even now, an unusually large percentage of the population has been indoctrinated and re-educated by the government schools, and for many of them, it will be the first time they have heard truth and common sense. There will be some who realize how blind they have been, but for most people it will just not make sense. Right now this show is just a novelty as well as being entertaining, but it will soon become the voice of reason and understanding, a voice for those who themselves are truth followers with common sense.

History is filled with those individuals that are truth haters, and it will be no exception in this case either. Most of the individuals that the program doesn't make sense to, will just turn it off, and go on their merry way, content to go through life unencumbered by higher thoughts, but some will understand that what is being aired is completely contradictory to their world view. This exposes their errant beliefs and lifestyles, but rather than embrace the truth, they will fight against it, even against all evidences.

As this fresh voice of sanity becomes more widely heard, his popularity will increase, and while he is relatively unheard of now, in just a few years, everyone will know who he is. This popularity will not mean that his ideas or conservatism are accepted, in fact the largest percentage of people will either hate or at the very least, detest him.

Americas love/hate relationship with this man, (for he will become larger than the program) will have a curious aspect to it, in that even those who dislike him will listen to the program religiously. Whether this is to find something he says and take it out of context, or simply morbid curiosity, they still will listen. Those who go beyond disliking and actually hate this man, will do so based on the erroneous reporting and sometimes outright falsifications of other media sources.

To understand the hatred this man will have to endure, and hatred it will be, one must understand the witless and absurd blindness that is called liberalism. In fact, it will be speaking out against the poison that is called liberalism, particularly as it pertains to the government, that will earn him this hostility. This hostility will only seem to fuel the show, and other programs modeled after this one, will be spawned, and conservative talk radio will have arrived.

When speaking about the poison of liberalism, the term needs to be defined, as there are some positive aspects in the strictest definition of liberal. It is those negative definitions which are being talked about. Rebels, socialists, indulgent, radical, non-conformist; all these describe liberals, as well as tolerant, understanding and permissive. These last three seem harmless enough, even compassionate, but in the world of liberalism, it is synonymous with acceptance, and there are some behaviors which should never be accepted or tolerated.

Liberalism, as this talk show will expose, is not so much concerned with individuals, as it is with government behavior. Your country was founded on such unique principles, as never seen before, and now there are forces within the system which are rebellious, socialist, indignant, radical and non-conformist. These are serious problems, and a government can only have these characteristics, when it is displayed against itself.

It is your constitution, which gives identity and guarantees stability to the country, but when individuals within the framework of government are actively opposed to this constitution, a loss of national identity and purpose creeps in. Whether these individuals are immoral activist judges, using their position to re-interpret the constitution based on so called evolving circumstances, or legislatures creating laws and bills designed to handcuff industries and citizens, or a president who compromises with these judges and legislatures; it is this type of illegal government behavior that is called liberalism.

Anyone who dares speak out against the corruption and unethical behavior of government and those responsible for this behavior, are bound to create powerful enemies, and this man will be no exception. In fact, were it not for some equally powerful allies, this program would not last for even five years. Though he is not aware of it, this mans most powerful ally, is in some respects also his enemy, for it is The Society which allows him to remain on the air.

In the next several years, he will have to endure several scandals, where his words will be taken out of context by his enemies, in an attempt to slander and demonize him, and his own actions will create a few scandals of their own, but his audience will be forgiving, and it will be as if it never happened.

One of the more comical of these attempts will come nearly twenty years from now, when the government itself will try and censure him for his opinions, but instead of using factual information, they will rely on what others have told them, rather than the truth. This endeavor to try and silence the free speech of a private citizen will backfire on those who had the audacity to attempt this, and it will be quite some time before they do it again.

This will just be another proof, that the citizens of your country have elected, and will continue to re-elect, individuals whose imbecilic behavior confirms a decline in morals. It will also reveal how much the poison of liberalism has infected the body of government.

Slanderous attacks will continue, as these are just the tip of the iceberg, and it would be ludicrous to enumerate every rumor and innuendo, but it all stems from the fact that those who practice liberalism cannot stand this man, and will do all they can to get him off the air. Why such hatred and contempt? Because he has the temerity to speak out against their immoral and illegal behavior, and bring their deeds to light.

Most of the people who attack him, are the very ones whom The Society has enabled to be in positions of leadership, (though in most cases they aren't aware of this fact), and the philosophies and tactics they use are in line with The Society's, so how can it be said that this Society is this mans biggest ally? To comprehend this, you must first know what their ultimate goal is, and who they are. All of this will be explained later, but for now, it must be understood that the poison of liberalism, is a tactic, not an end in itself.

For the most part, those who claim to be liberals and spout liberal propaganda, are simply deluded dreamers, whose minds have wandered into the opiate fields of fantasy. However, it is in these fields of fantasy where fantastic and fanatical theories such as man made global warming and oil shortages are hatched, and these two theories will cause much anxiety, and will have to be dealt with early in the next century.

But its not all about liberalism versus conservatism, and while this is an important aspect of the programming, there are two main reasons why the show will continue year after year. The first reason, is that it will generate a large amount of income.

While there are many facets to the media, it needs to be examined as a whole, for its sole purpose is as a tool for propaganda, and economic gain. True, it does impart useful facts like the weather, obituaries and other such information, but these are really inducements for people to be involved in the acceptance of media, and to legitimize their existence, rather than a purpose for being. Economics rules the day when it comes to which is more important, but many times the line between it and propaganda is so thin, that it is like asking which came first, the chicken or the egg?

Economics is the driving force in nearly all forms of media, and programming is designed foremost in order to attract large audiences that will listen to advertising. True, television is a great tool to use for propaganda, but if it were not for entertainment drawing viewers into watching ads, television would soon cease. Entertainment is solely for money, nothing else. Just twenty years from now, advertisers will be willing to spend several million dollars to run a thirty second ad in one of your sports championships. If this sporting event did not generate such large amounts of money, something else would be aired. If watching grass grow created large advertising revenue, it would be televised instead.

This is one of the main reasons that this conservative talk radio host is allowed to continue. He produces large sums of advertising revenue. More importantly however, is the fact that he is divisive, and keeps conservatives and liberals at odds with one another.

Whenever a government or organization desires complete dominance over the hearts and minds of its subjects, it must create a common cause or enemy to fight against. The truthfulness of the cause is irrelevant, and one of the greatest examples of this occurred just fifty years ago in Germany. Through concerted propaganda efforts, the people were united against a common enemy, and this small country was able to accomplish great feats, even though they were evil, and inhumane.

Today, in America, that specific enemy is truth and righteousness, synonymous with conservatism, and this minority is seen as the perfect scapegoat. In the years to come, this antagonism between conservatives and liberals will only escalate, and unfortunately, the lies and poison of liberalism, will replace truth. Truth demands responsibility, and people are increasingly being taught, whether in government schools, or media, that they are not personally responsible for their actions, and the government can and will be their nurse maid from cradle to grave. This will create great chasms of divisiveness; truth, justice and responsibility, against the lie of immorality, laziness, and the overindulgence of self interest.

Exposing the lies of such propaganda, and stirring up truth in the minds of the people will begin to have an affect, and more and more people will realize the thievery and treason that has been perpetuated against them. Thieves posing as government well doers, will redistribute the wealth they have garnished from the citizens, and those who understand what is happening will loath and detest what is transpiring in their once great republic. No moral government can take from one citizen and give to another without becoming likened as a common thief, and thief and recipient alike are treasonous, and therefore should be treated as such. Those who participate in this scheme should be treated as traitors, and given the punishment deserved.

However, government schools have so thoroughly indoctrinated thief and recipient alike, that they feel the welfare state is not only legitimate, but that they are entitled to the resources they receive, and anyone who exposes them for what they are will incur their hatred. The number of individuals receiving entitlements is quite large, and in the years to come will only increase. They do not know they have been enslaved in the chains of liberalism, and when conservatives show it for what it is, these slaves become fearful that their entitlements might get taken away, and resent any attempt to free them.

Right now the voice of conservatism is relatively small, but by 2000, it will start to make an impact, and while The Society desires the enslavement of humanity, using liberalism to poison the mind, and conservative talk radio to create divisiveness, it will be necessary for them to quell and subdue conservatism before it grows into a force to large to deal with.

From 1949 until last year, 1987, a rule known as the fairness doctrine was in place so that if need be, views contrary to popular opinion could not be silenced, but primarily it was used to silence views that might expose the illegal or morally suspicious actions of those in positions of authority. The constitutionality of such a rule was dubious at best, and was finally overturned in 1987.

In the years to come, there will be several attempts to reinstate this rule, usually by those who are unscrupulous members of your congress. Twenty years from now, the attempts to renew this will be relentless, and though it will take several more years after this to get it into effect, it will be back, and conservative talk radio will begin to be silenced. It will take several lawsuits and imprisonments, but eventually these shows will become economic liabilities, and will begin to dwindle out of sight.

No longer will people feel or think that conservatism is relative to life, and in 2025 the show that began it all, the lone survivor, will go off the air. For nearly four decades, these voices will be warning of the dangers and destructiveness of liberalism, out of control governments, and immoral behavior, but in the end, they will be silenced, just another whisper in the annals of history; the poison of liberalism will have worked its magic.

CHAPTER 13

Educational indoctrination into the tenets of liberalism, and media disinformation are excellent means in which to enslave mankind, but economic enslavement completes the package. It is not only more powerful than education and media combined, but it is so subtle, that its impact on society is rarely realized until it is too late, and even then most people will not understand what is happening.

For ease of discussion, this chronicle will use the two monetary terms, finance and economics, interchangeably, and it is more important that the reader understand the significance economics plays and has played in the history of mankind, than the miniscule differences in definitions.

While it is almost impossible to explain the significance economics has had in the affairs of man without mentioning some of the history behind it, even this brief history will be incomplete, and will perhaps leave more unanswered questions, than answers. Economics delves into so many areas, that it will not be prudent to mention them all, but it is important that the reader of this chronicle understands enough, so that the entirety of it all might be grasped.

Almost from the beginning, man has used financial tools as a means of obtaining power and control over others, and this is where the aspect of enslavement subtly comes in.

Cain, the firstborn of your original parents, was taught the secret knowledge of finance, by one of the fallen watchers, who was skilled in the art of mathematics, and Cain was given this knowledge in order that his own life might be one of ease and comfort, exploiting the toil of others, and thereby circumventing his punishment for rebelling against the Creator. Exploiting another persons labor is just another way of seizing their resources, without resorting to force and violence, and if the masses willingly hand over these resources so much the better. This is where the aspect of subjugation becomes apparent. Although speculation and indebtedness will be the major tools used in this subjugation, it is in fact the greed and lust for luxury and power that will place the chains on the lives of men. Rare is the individual who is content with his lot in life.

Using violence and the knowledge he had been given, Cain was able to control a large portion of the world that was inhabited at the time, as were the sons he passed this information to upon his death. Nonetheless, all this wisdom and enlightenment was lost as a result of the great deluge, and it was several generations afterward, when once again man increased upon the face of the earth, that this knowledge was given to another. This individual was not only given the secrets of financial exploitation, but other mysteries that had been forbidden for humans to learn. He used this information so well, that the kingdom he built is still considered a marvel to the current day, and some of the ruins from this ancient culture can still be seen. If his name were revealed, it would be immediately recognized, but the watchers are forbidden to speak of who he was, or any specific feats he accomplished.

Eventually, this man also died, but not before indoctrinating another into the mysteries and secrets of finance, and relinquishing all assets to this individual. This scenario repeated itself for many generations, each one becoming wealthier and more powerful, but as mankind spread throughout the earth, and increased in number, it became necessary to instruct and prepare others to rule this secret empire. Currently there are ten men in this Society, and while there were fewer in the past, the need for more than ten will never arise, for they have divided the world into five economic regions; two men for each region.

One of the men in each of these five groups is an apprentice, so in some respects there are only five who actually control the different world economies. Currently there is a concerted effort to conglomerate the countries within these regions into economic unions, with a common currency. The first of these to have any significance will be the European Union, and though it will become official in just five years, it will be nearly 2002, before a common currency is minted and put into circulation.

These five men are the heads, but as in any large organization, there are many individuals involved in the daily operations of this colossal enterprise, and many smaller organizations within the whole. There is one overseer that advises these men, and directs their actions when necessary, and it is the same fallen watcher that has been leading the Society since the time of Cain. This watcher's desire is that all of mankind be enslaved, and the motives of he and his fallen brethren will be explained in more detail later in the chronicle.

Though there are many hidden agendas within the scope of economic activity, it does have a very useful and necessary function. It is nearly impossible for a barter type system to work on a large scale, so as man spread out upon the earth, and increased in number, it was necessary for some type of monetary system to be invented. Even during the time of Cain, nearly every village had its own monetary system, and in most cases it was just a glorified barter system with some type of common standard on which to base trade. As villages merged into regions, and regions into nations, it became even more necessary to have some type of standard, and in nearly all cases, this was a measured weight of gold.

There are several reasons why gold was primarily used, but several other mediums were popular also. Silver, a variety of precious stones, and several other industrial type metals like copper, lead and bronze were used, and sometimes even more exotic things like ivory and perfumes were utilized in trade.

In the progression of time, societies that were primarily agriculturally based became diversified, and goods and services, along with various industries, necessitated a need for gold to be broken into smaller trading units, so coinage was invented. Eventually, paper money was introduced, but in all instances, this money had a specific set value based on gold.

This is a very brief and rudimentary explanation of the beginnings of finance and economics, and since volumes have been and will continue to be written on this subject, the reader wishing to gain additional knowledge in this area, has plenty of literature to choose from.

Speculation and indebtedness, as stated earlier, are tools used to inflame lust and greed, and these lusts and greed are such driving forces within the human psyche, that it is virtually impossible to unchain oneself from these influences, once they have taken hold. Much study has been done on why this is, but it can be simplified, in order that an understanding of the ease in which man is enslaved can be seen.

After mans corruption, death entered the world, and there was such a sense of helplessness and despair, that man turned to hope, but instead of turning his attention to the true source of hope, he allowed lust and greed to be his ruler. In every generation, there has been the idea, that by having more wealth and power, an individual will have more control over his circumstances, subconsciously thinking they can cheat death.

Man does not know where this hopelessness came from, or when it began, (there are a few who do, but as a whole, mankind does not) but I will impart a bit of wisdom to the reader who cares to know. Meditate on this carefully, and perhaps the light of understanding will illuminate your mind, and hopelessness will flee. The driving force behind all human endeavor and motivations, is the fear of death. No more will be said on this, but the men in the Society understand this fear, and have been using it to exploit mankind for thousands of years.

Under normal economic circumstances, industry and trade will grow, but at a very slow rate, and at a rate where everyone will benefit. This does not mean that everyone will have the same standard of living, but everyone will be sufficiently compensated for their work, and have the necessities of life; food, clothing and shelter. This type of society generally lacks very little, and usually has excesses that can be used in a variety of ways.

Yet this rarely happens, and the few times it has, it did not last long. Because of the economic freedoms you have enjoyed in the United States, the situation is still very favorable there, and nearly all have their needs met, and many have surpluses which are being used to expand industry.

Large numbers of people can live sufficiently in such an environment, and the few who do lack the means in which to earn an income, are taken care of by charitable means. However, economic freedom and humanitarianism are not in the best interest of the Society, and by using the tools of speculation and credit, it is their desire to have only a small percentage of people with sufficient means to support themselves without the help of the government.

Since this chronicle deals primarily with the United States, very little will be said about the situations in other countries, but nearly all of their economies have been taken over by the Society, and third world countries will never advance except in superficial ways, and are irrelevant. When I say these economies have been taken over, it is really two economies running at the same time, one seen, and one not, and though they are both real, one of them is actually an artificial system.

It is very difficult to explain how two systems can operate simultaneously, and for one of them to remain unnoticed, and the other one to be artificial, but to help explain it in a very elementary way, examples from the popular board game, Monopoly, will be used.

Usually there are several players, and the object of the game is to buy, sell and trade properties, in an attempt to generate revenue, and to create situations where your opponent will go bankrupt. Other than generating revenue through properties, there is a type of salary one gets for completing a revolution around the board, but this is generally only enough to complete another revolution, not create wealth. When a player becomes bankrupt, he is out of the game, and the last surviving player is declared the winner. For most players, this is just a game, but it is a fascinating game when one looks at the manipulation, luck and psychology involved.

Suppose however, that instead of allowing, or forcing a player to quit the game, no one can leave, and they can borrow money as needed, with interest of course, and if anything catastrophic happens, like landing on an expensive property, they will be allowed to go further into debt. Since the income derived from completing a revolution around the game board will never pay off the debt, the player will eventually go deeper and deeper into indebtedness.

Another scenario is that a player may have enough property, and generate enough income, to stay in a state of consistency, never gaining much, but never losing anything either. There is no possibility of winning or losing, just an endless repetition around the board. Eventually, tiring of the game, they will, through a series of bad moves or trades, lose the game, or in the event of good trades win. But, since no one can quit, they are in the same situation as the first scenario, unless they happen to be the one winning.

The third possibility, or scenario, is that the person who

would have won the game if it were played in a normal manner, allows a rule change where the income received for completing a revolution is increased. Since the winner owns all the property, this would allow the other players from going further into debt, and at the same time insure steady revenue for the property holder. This would also allow play to continue in a smooth manner, but without the possibility of anyone replacing the winner.

Now to continue this analogy, the winner, or controller, for want of a better word, decides that the game has become monotonous, and gives one of the players a salary, and perhaps the benefit of temporary property ownership, to play the game for him, so that he can attend to other matters. This controller is still a player, but allows this other individual to do all the work involved in the game.

This works fine for a while, but since no player can leave, and there is a finite amount of money, eventually it will run out. At this point, the controller changes the game again, and arranges to run the bank, for a fee, and to print additional money to loan the bank as the need arises. Essentially, the bank which originally facilitated play between players, and was neutral to the game, has become the property of the controller, and he now controls distributions, and receives funds, and instead of being neutral, the bank has now become a source of income.

In the game, the original money has a value based on the houses, hotels and properties within the game, but any additional printed money introduced to the game, will only have a value based on a percentage of the original. Whenever additional money is put into the game, it creates a situation in which the values of the property go up, as well as rental fees, and it becomes necessary to again raise income, but since the rise in income never keeps up with rising property values, the players are in a constant state of debt. Eventually, this never ending cycle of rising values, along with the increase in printed money, causes such disarray, that the game becomes pointless, and is over. For those players who were in a perpetual state of indebtedness, nothing really has changed, for they were being carried by the other players, much like government welfare does, but for the few players who managed to keep their head above water, all is over.

Unfortunately for the players in our scenario, the game must go on, so a new monetary system is developed and put into play, but all assets, and the real money (original money) are still owned by the one player, so even with this new system, nothing has really changed. Now to continue this analogy, suppose the game goes on for not just a lifetime, but for several generations.

All of the original players, including the controller, have long since passed away, but since the controller passed all his assets to a single player, everything remains the same, and since it has been this way for so long, it seems normal.

Most of the players are in a state of perpetual servant hood, and perhaps one or two have obtained an artificial type of self sufficiency, but the only one who really knows what is going on, and what the game is about, is the controller who has been given this knowledge by his predecessor. The only real way to progress and get ahead, is to obtain some of the original currency, or property, but except under very rare conditions, the controller will never allow this to happen.

This is a very crude and rudimentary example of what is really happening, and how two sets of economies are existing at the same time. The artificial one that takes place in the day to day existence of everyday life; bill paying, jobs, income, the occasional taste of luxury, the existence that nearly everyone experiences, and then the real economy that is being played out behind the scenes over decades, lifetimes, even centuries.

When America was young, and principles designed to keep such a scenario from taking place were made into laws, economic freedom was available to all. Not everyone took advantage of this opportunity, but it was there nonetheless, and millions from other countries, immigrated to the United States, seeking the American dream.

It was understood by your founding fathers, that a central bank, personal income taxes and personal property taxes were tools to enslave people, and if the true freedom that was given to all men by the Creator was to prevail, government could never have these tools at their disposal. With principles such as these, the republic grew strong, and even a civil war did not destroy these freedoms, and it was nearly 150 years before immoral men began changing the laws.

Early in the 1900s, laws were changed and enacted, in order to enslave the American people, and after much re-education, propaganda and time, the people have for the most part accepted this situation. Nearly everyone believes that the government has the right to take from its citizens, and few realize the devastation it has caused.

When the citizens allowed the government to enact private property taxes, they were in effect, giving full ownership of the nations land into the hands of those who operate the government. Much like our game scenario, one party owns the land, and leases it out at varying rates, and charges nominal fees, but never relinquishes ownership. There are those who will scoff at this notion, but try not paying your taxes, and see what becomes of your land.

Maybe now the devastation that government education and media have produced is beginning to sink in, for how else could people allow themselves to be so easily duped like this. Personal income taxes, was just another ruse to relieve people of their assets, but the most damaging was the formation of a central bank. Again referring to our game reference, this is just a sham to keep real assets from rarely being owned by the general public, and eventually the continued printing of money without sufficient collateral to back it up, will collapse the economy.

Originally, that universal common standard, gold, was used to back the printed money, but much more was printed then there was gold to back it up, yet the U.S. economy remained strong. With America being the last truly free country in the world, (though you are losing many rights quickly), and being the powerful nation it is, other means were necessary to reduce the citizens to docile cattle.

This will be accomplished in several different ways, and while all of them are in their infancy stage, the havoc they will cause upon reaching maturity, will be catastrophic. The most

important step, though it wasn't the first, was when your 37th
president took your paper currency off the gold standard. Though it
has only been seventeen years, already it has caused problems of
inflation, and artificial government restrictions. Though this
president is given credit for doing this, it wasn't really his decision
to make, but he was told to do this by those who own the central
bank. Later, in the section on politics, it will become clearer, that
government isn't necessarily a power unto itself, but the functions
that it has, and the functions it can create, have the real power.

Two other major steps going on right now, and increasing
at a phenomenal rate, are speculation under the guise of
investment, and indebtedness which is just another word for credit.
While credit is just a word to ease the negative connotations that
the word debt has, just fifteen to twenty years from now, people
will desire to be credit worthy, not realizing being in debt is not
something to be strived for. Before going any further into the
details of credit and speculation, another event needs to be
mentioned, and that is your Social Security program. Because it
will eventually affect the investment markets, and to a certain
degree credit, it needs to be examined.

Originally introduced as a retirement safety net, it ensured
that the elderly would not live in poverty, and if someone became

disabled, there would be a steady source of income. In short, it enabled those individuals to pay their bills, and have something to eat, without being a burden on the state, or anyone else. However, in reality it has become one of the most elaborate Ponzi schemes ever perpetuated upon mankind.

By using actuary scales, it was set up in a way that in most cases, people died before receiving many benefits, and as the population increased, so did revenues. With the introduction of inflation, it became necessary to pay recipients more, as well as raise S.S. taxes, or contributions as they are humorously called.

All this surplus revenue was kept in a discretionary account, but when it finally reached a predetermined value, it was in effect stolen by certain members within the government. This was done by taking the money in the trust fund, or discretionary account, and then issuing special government bonds to replace the money. Basically this is a loan, but all the parties involved knew it was nothing more than sleight of hand thievery.

This thievery continues to go on today, and will continue to go on until the Social Security program is disbanded. It will continue to go on for at least another twenty five years, but not much longer than that, and while it appears strong right now, as the population lives longer, and fewer people are around to pay into the system, major changes will have to be made. It will become necessary to raise the age at which people can retire, and also will necessitate a raise in taxation. Couple this with the continuing rise in inflation, and like our game analogy, it must collapse.

This Ponzi scheme was initiated in 1935, and just over fifty years later, it is having its desired effect. If the brilliance of the minds who hatched this scheme, had been channeled toward good instead of evil, think what may have been accomplished. Unfortunately, another Ponzi type scheme will be introduced in the not to distant future, and will be initially called universal health care. It will take 30-40 years before it will actually become a reality, but once it does, it will be the end of the greatest health care system on earth. This will work out great for controlling the population, and the social security problem, but that is all that will be mentioned about this scheme.

Since the introduction of social security, people no longer feel the need to save excess income for their retirement years, and instead of investing for the future, begin to speculate. Most of this will be done in your stock markets, though some will venture into the commodities and similar get rich gimmicks, but as a whole, the bulk of investment will go into the stock market. The difference between speculation and investment, is that generally, speculation is much riskier and has greater potential for reward, where investing is a slow and methodical way of increasing wealth. Since most people will be placing their money into the stock market, that is the area that will be discussed.

On the surface, stocks as a whole seem to be a great way to invest in the development of a company, or participate in its growth and profitability, and if one approaches it in that manner, and carefully chooses financially healthy corporations, it may in time, through dividends and price growth, prove to be a wise investment.

However, most people do not choose in this manner, but allow salesmen whose income depends on commissions, and who generally have little training, to choose for them. The sheer number of stocks to choose from intimidates most people, so instead of investigating and finding those healthy corporations, it is hit and miss, and usually miss. In the next twenty years, the number to choose from will increase dramatically, and with the explosion of the personal computer, several new industries will spring up, elevating the number even higher.

Not only will the number of individual stocks increase, but so will the number of mutual funds and derivatives. Mutual funds and derivatives will actually be a major factor for the large number of people who will enter the markets, for they will feel these products are safer because of the diversification they allow.

Twenty years ago, there were just over three hundred funds to choose from, but now there is nearly three thousand, and in another twenty years there will be over eight thousand. This will create a situation where diversification is still safe, but not nearly as safe as in the past. As more money flows into these funds, the principal of supply and demand will kick in, and it will artificially inflate the price of individual stocks. Instead of people investing in company performance, they will be speculating on the idea that the demand will continue to cause the rise in the value of their fund.

The public will become so enamored with this type of investing, that there will even be mutual funds consisting of a basket of other mutual funds. Eventually, reality will come crashing in, as will the market, and trillions will be lost. This will not occur until the 2020s, so for those desiring to do so, there is plenty of time to profit from this situation, but be warned, this is just paper, and will dissolve into thin air. The crash is inevitable, but this build up has taken place over a number of years, in order that more money might be placed into the markets.

When this crash occurs, it will resemble three other catastrophes of the past; the tulip bulb mania, the Mississippi

Company bubble and the South Sea bubble. The greatest difference between these three and your stock market crash will be the time frame in which it happened. This market crash will have been orchestrated over many years, in order that when it does happen, no one will suspect that it had been planned in advance, and having learned from the past, the Society realizes more can be accomplished in this area over a period of years, then allowing it to happen in just a short period of time.

However, hard assets such as land, real estate, precious metals and even just cash in the bank, will not generate the income that the stock market will make in the next twenty years, and as more people realize this, and the media promotes it, the market will climb even higher. Right now, your main index is just a little over 2000, after taking a plunge last year, and this will keep some people from ever returning to the market, (this is an intended act, which will be explained momentarily,) but in just ten years, it will have quadrupled to around 8000, and in just another ten years, will have hit 14000. There will be dips along the way, one or two quite severe, but the market will recover quite quickly.

These severe dips, coincide with a tragic event in one case, and war in the other, but in actuality, these events were used to manipulate the market. This has happened many times in the past, and like the bubbles that were mentioned earlier, were planned events. These have a two fold effect, one being that when the market bounces back after one of these dips, people tend to have more confidence in the overall stability and strength of the market, and will invest even more, but the second effect is somewhat more sinister.

Each time the market makes one of these sharp downturns, there are a number of people who either lose everything they have invested, or decide to cut their loses and get out of the market entirely. In most cases, theses individuals will never enter the market again, and generally never make another attempt to save or make any extra money. This will be especially noticeable after the stock market crash of 2008, and its subsequent recovery.

This money they have lost represents time out of their life, and because these dips were purpose driven, it means that someone has in effect stolen this time, and these people have worked for free, or as it were, as slaves. Tragically, many others do not realize this, and continue to put large amounts of their resources into the markets, and will never know that they have been working as slaves, for wages which they will never use or see again. They have been chained by their greed for more, and though the markets have been, and will continue to be manipulated by the Society, it will ultimately be that greedy individual who has placed the chains of self induced slavery upon their life.

Much more could be said about the market, and how fear and greed can be used to manipulate peoples actions, but this is just a snapshot of what is going on, and in the 2020s when it crashes, trillions upon trillions of dollars, representing thousands of lifetimes of work, will have vanished into thin air.

Not everyone has resources in which to invest or speculate, but they have greed and lusts that desire to be satisfied, and through credit this craving will be satisfied. This ease with which people will be able to obtain credit, will be the greatest enslaver of all time, and it is just now starting to accelerate at an exponential rate. While economic manipulations have always been the Society's greatest means in which to enslave mankind, credit is and always has been the most important tool in which to do this. It is so detrimental to society, that in the great chronicle that the Creator gave to the human race, He warned that the borrower would be servant to the lender, but who has heeded such wisdom?

In times past, being in debt had a negative connotation, and ordinary people only did so under most severe circumstances, and even then were reluctant to, but now every type of purchase, regardless of need, can be had on credit. This is not only an individual problem but a social problem, for your government is spending itself into oblivion.

Not that long ago, people were buying their automobiles with cash, sometimes even their homes, and if a mortgage was necessary, it was for a short of term as possible, rarely more than fifteen years. That is not the case anymore, and credit companies try and get the longest time payment possible. This generates more interest income, and since payments are generally lower, it is easier to convince consumers to borrow larger amounts. In the not to distant future, cars will be financed for up to seven years, and homes will have forty year mortgages.

Credit will be something everyone strives for, and it will be given a favorable status, but it is still just debt that has to be repaid. Very few people will escape this devastating phenomenon, and with these credit companies targeting the youngest users, it will be rare that anyone of legal age isn't in perpetual debt. From student loans and consumer debt, to an added mortgage, individuals will be in debt from the moment they enter the job market, until they retire, and they will have spent their entire adult life in slavery.

The government is even less responsible, and the debt it is piling up will eventually destroy the foundations of your republic, and it will then be possible for the Society to easily step in and present solutions. Ten years ago your national debt was around one trillion, now it is nearly three trillion, and will be nearly ten trillion just twenty years from now. The national debt coupled with personal debt, will reach such heights, that it will never be repaid.

There will be those who argue that the great economic boom that America has experienced was built on the foundation of credit, and in a sense this is correct, but this foundation was built by slaves called Americans, and which is more tragic, the eventual collapse of a artificial economic system and its currency, or continued slavery.

Thousands of books have been written on economics, finance and the way it is integrated into society, and it is impossible for this chronicle to touch every area it affects, but for those interested, the role gold and central banks play would be worth studying further.

The collapse of your economy and currency will occur approximately thirty five years from now, and there is no avoiding it, and although various attempts to curtail this disaster will be made, the damage created by the central bank and its subsidiaries will be irreversible. Because these central banks are all related, or owned by those controlled by the Society, it will be necessary from time to time for all of them to work in synchronicity.

An example of this will occur approximately twenty years from now, when many credit institutions become insolvent, and central banks from around the world, inject trillions into the market systems, in order that they do not collapse. By all of these banks doing it at the same time, it is not seen as inflationary, as it would be if just one or two did it. This and your government taking over several major institutions will postpone the inevitable, but a collapse must come. The seignorage generated will have been siphoned off into real assets of land and precious metals, and like our game analogy, a new system will be created, but all true assets will be owned by one individual, or in this case, The Society.

CHAPTER 14

Without the cooperation of government entities, none of the previous mentioned institutions would be able to function in a coordinated way, and their ability to enslave the minds and souls of citizens, would be greatly hampered. However, it is not the government itself that is the culprit, but individuals within, who use the functions within government for either political gain, or just raw power. Indeed, many of these individuals are themselves under the authority of those who have made it possible for them to be in positions of leadership.

Another problem is that the populace has forgotten that the United States is a republic, not a democracy, and have elected leaders who are not only immoral, but unqualified as well. This lack of qualification makes it extremely easy for these individuals to be manipulated by more experienced members of the government, and the results are usually devastating.

This decay did not occur overnight, and though it started in earnest nearly seventy five years ago, elements of destruction had already crept in. By the turn of the century it will have grown even worse, in fact, people will wonder how it ever was allowed to get that bad. Citizens will question the motives of these politicians, knowing that there is no logical, or at least ethical, reason behind many of the decisions they make. It will get to the point, that not long before the 2008 elections, confidence in the government will reach an all time low.

Unfortunately, no country has allowed their government to become this decadent, and then have it become right again, and yours is no exception. By 2020, it will be unrecognizable to the way it was only 150 years ago, and there is no turning back.

At the present moment, and for the next twenty five years, there is the ability to change, for not all rights have been stripped away, but not enough people see what is happening, and those who do, are powerless to change the direction this poison of liberalism has gone.

There is time to educate a generation on how a republic works, replace those who work immorality in your government, and take down some of the destructive bureaucracies that exist, but it is not going to happen.

Chronicles do not always present a pleasant scenario, but they do testify that something could have been done about certain situations, but usually nothing is changed, as the reader is either powerless, or apathetic to the situation.

As mentioned earlier in the chronicle, this year, 1988, is the last year of a truly elected president, and all the rest will be hand picked by the Society, and though there may be some cosmetic differences between candidates, they all have one master. The media will increasingly play a larger role in the picking of this head of government, and it will reach a point where the line between celebrities and politicians, is difficult to distinguish.

Since it will still be approximately forty years before presidential elections are done away with, (they will be chosen by your senate and house, from among their members) much attention will be given to the candidates, but no one outside your two established political parties will be allowed much credence, and it will be said that a vote for a third party, is a wasted vote. This is not true of course, but truth and truthfulness will be virtually non existent in these elections.

Even though these presidents are the peoples only choice,

hence really no choice at all, they are only the figure head of the government, and while they are powerful, the real power lies behind those who put their resources into getting these men elected. It is not only the president that they are interested in, but many others in your congress have been selected for positions of power, in order that all government functions might be more easily manipulated.

Usually this is simply an individual whose desire for power and influence clouds his judgment, and has become an easy target for those who will get him elected. Once elected, it is simply a matter of reminding this individual from time to time, of how they got their position, and that if they wish to continue in that position, they will do the bidding of their benefactor. Most times there is no coercion, just a simple desire that certain legislation be voted on in a particular way, or perhaps even introducing legislation beneficial to the interests of their backers.

Then there are the more sinister individuals, who have some dark secret in their past, or present, and out of fear, will do the bidding of those who help them get elected. In either case, once elected and having tasted the nectar of power and the pleasures accompanying it, most politicians are quite willing to sell their souls to retain this power.

Occasionally, there will be an individual who makes it to the federal level of government, who is responsible, has moral integrity, and places the priorities of the country in its proper perspective, but try as they may to overcome the corruption, very little is accomplished, and they become disillusioned and quit, or assimilate into the system.

Less than a decade from now, one of your political parties will release what it calls a contract with America, and while this appears to be a chance to bring back integrity, morality, responsibility and accountability, it will actually accomplish very little of this. Even this concerted effort will do little to stem the tide of corruption, and twenty years from now, it will have no noticeable impact.

Very little will be said about government at the local and state level, but in most instances, its personality is very similar to that of the federal government, and since those at the federal level have come through the ranks of these lower institutions, it is clear that most of them are corrupt also.

To those desiring truly effective and lasting changes in the morality of government, it will be necessary to rid yourselves of the corruption you have allowed at the local level, otherwise, it is futile to attempt to do so at higher levels.

Before moving on, it should be noted, that whenever an election comes during a critical time, whether it is war or some economic downturn, the difference between the two candidates will be greatly exaggerated. Even though most of this is orchestrated, this great difference is used in order that a particular candidate will be chosen.

You will notice this to a certain degree in your 1992 elections, when the incumbent president is ousted by a relative unknown liberal governor. This outsider is chosen to win for a variety of reasons, but primarily for a slip of the tongue by the president, when he mentions the idea of a new world order. This new world order is coming, and will be mentioned later, but the timing was not right for the public to be introduced to this concept, and it was deemed necessary to remove the president before a second term.

This diversity will be particularly noticeable in your 2000 and 2008 elections, so much in fact, that after the 2008 elections, one party's integrity will be called into question. By allowing an inexperienced and naïve candidate to be their presidential nominee, one whose principles were very anti-american, they will become not only the laughingstock of leaders from around the world, but discrepancies in voting numbers will lead to charges of fraud. This will all take place behind closed doors, in order that the public doesn't see the rampant chaos in this particular party, and after the election, all charges will be dropped.

Many of the leaders who laugh at this individual, will secretly desire that he wins the presidency, for he will be a push over for their every demand, but inwardly they know, that the final decision lies with the Society.

This debacle and one similar to it in 2016, will be travesty enough, but after violent deaths and several bombings related to the 2020 party conventions, it will be clear that too much time and money is being spent on presidential elections. Media will begin a campaign to instill the idea that congress is more qualified to choose a national leader than the public, and within two years, the public is ready.

However, there will still be some pockets of resistance, and it will take the assassination of the favored candidate in the spring of 2027, before final action is taken. With no constitutional grounds, or national vote, congress mandates that presidential elections cease, and the national leader be chosen from among members of the senate.

Though there is no constitutional means to do this, the members of the Supreme court, long filled with liberal idealists desiring to do away with the constitution, agree with the congress, and in one fell swoop, will effectively do away with one branch of the government.

For many years, the effectiveness and power of the presidency had been waning, so while this will seem to be devastating and destructive, very little difference will be noticed. The destruction comes from the disintegration of your constitution, and the America just forty years from now, will be so in name only.

By having hand picked individuals in positions of leadership, the Society has in essence been able to take over the functions of the government, and this is where true power lies. By creating agencies and bureaucracies with very little accountability, abuses of power can run rampant, and many laws or regulations by fiat are created. This will be particularly noticeable in the 1990s, but two particular sets of regulations will be noted, as they will have tremendous impact, not only nationally, but globally.

The first instance has to do with energy regulations, and many of these regulations have already been put into place, and the second has to do with the myth of man made global warming. Right now there is little to no concern with climate change, but after the turn of the century, it will start to become a primary issue.

This will be in large part due to one particular individual, whose mind has become so entwined with liberalism and self importance, that leaving logic behind, becomes fully engrossed in this religion of earth worship.

Little does he know, but this fantasy of his was suggested to him years ago, and it is the only way he can retain even the remotest semblance of power. This myth is being used to keep certain assets in the hands of a small group, who ironically were able to seize them by using those energy regulations of the 1970s and 1980s.

Most of the regulations having to do with climate change will not take effect until after 2010, but they are directly related to the energy regulations of four decades earlier.

For his part in creating a sense of urgency out of this myth, the Society will arrange for this individual to receive a prestigious award, forever staining the reputation of the organization presenting him with this award.

These two situations, energy and climate, will be discussed in the section dealing with the oil wars, that will be coming in about twenty years, but they are just a brief example of how government functions under the control of the Society, can be bent to their will.

Using government agencies to do their bidding, is also useful when it is becomes necessary to shift accountability from the private sector, to the government. Twenty years from now, just two months before the presidential election, the United States government will take over two failing mortgage companies, in an effort to ease global concerns over credit instability. This will effectively increase the debt liability of the country by several trillion dollars, and while it is welcomed by financial institutions around the globe, it is only a temporary solution, which will not be solved. Weeks later, a similar situation will arise, and though billions of dollars are also thrown at this problem, it is not understood that this is a moral problem, not monetary, and it too will fail and usher in the market crash of 2008.

As illustrated before in our game analogy, this has all been planned, and a global financial collapse, led by the United States, will occur within two decades after this mortgage farce, and a new and global financial system will be initiated.

Eventually, all governments will be consolidated into one, and even now it is in place, but without any real power. You know it as the United Nations, and while it does function and act like a government, it has no independent military force, or taxing power, and must rely on donations to operate, and any military actions it undertakes, is simply a coalition of units from its member nations. At the present time, it is the United States that stands in the way of this entity from becoming a single government in control over all the world, and this is the cause of many of the anti-american views that will become prevalent among members of your own congress in the next twenty years. These members believe that a one world government is the next step in the development of the human race, and will do all in their power to see it become a reality.

The Society has complete control over the operation of the United Nations, picks its leaders, and is just waiting until it becomes a viable institution, before enacting some very restrictive regulations, which will in essence end human freedom as expressed in your United States constitution. This will all take place in 2029, after a new world monetary system has been started, and though it has taken nearly 7000 years, the Society will have finally succeeded in completely controlling all aspects of human life, but one, which will be further discussed later in the chronicle.

CHAPTER 15

Before this final globalization takes place, several seemingly unrelated events take place, but they are integral parts of what will come to be known as the oil wars. These oil wars will be as much economic and philosophical as they are military, and most of the time, the lines between enemy and ally are difficult to determine. They could also be called religious wars, as will be explained later, and while there will be many independent battles, it is in reality just one long continuous war.

But before the oil wars are discussed, there is an epidemic that is going on right now, and will continue to grow, that must be mentioned. It was first recognized just seven years ago, and has become known by the term Aids. This virus called human immunodeficiency virus, or HIV, leads to what will be known as

AIDS, or the acquired immunodeficiency syndrome. What is unique about this virus, is that there is no effective cure, and it was an experiment gone bad.

The virus was first discovered in the 1930s by those studying primates, but was not seriously looked at until the 1950s, when certain scientists determined to finding a easily transmittable biological disease, stumbled across the earlier research. These were not government or military scientists, but opportunists seeking to develop a time released virus, capable of destroying entire nations. It was their intention, to sell this biological weapon to the highest bidder, but errors in the development of the time release agent, caused the virus to spread in the early 1980s, fifteen years before planned.

These scientists had perfected this virus, so that it would be transferred from one individual to another, primarily through sexual relations, but the effects wouldn't show up until years later. Their plan was to infect approximately twenty five members of the homosexual community, and when the virus activated fifteen years later, the numbers infected by their promiscuous lifestyle, would be staggering. Such an authentic experiment as this, would fetch them billions of dollars, but a miscalculation in the timing agent, caused the infection to break out less than a year after the men had been contaminated with this disease. They decided to scrap everything, but the harm had been done, and just seven years later, the numbers infected, are over half a million. Twenty years from now, the numbers will be in the millions, and growing, with nearly three quarters of the infected, living on the continent of Africa.

There is no evidence that there will have been a concerted effort to infect Africa, and all that is allowed to be said on this subject is to look at the natural resources this continent contains, and who might benefit from the destruction of nearly all life on this large land mass.

The only reason this epidemic is mentioned, is to let the reader know that there will be two more major disease outbreaks, both involving flu strains, and they will have been specifically designed to eradicate large numbers of people from off the earth. The first will occur in 2025, and though it will be very short in duration, less than a year, over two billion people will die in this epidemic. The second will occur nearly 10 years later, and a similar number of people will die, but it will last for three years. Both of these flu strains will have been time released, and the half million or so people originally infected, will have been given these strains in 2008.

This little excursion into the details of these pandemics,

does not seem to have any bearing with the oils wars, and very few will ever make the connection, but it is somewhat related, as will be mentioned later.

Even before the Society set up the United Nations, or even before its first failed attempt called the League of Nations, they knew that eventually the worlds population would reach a point, that natural resources would not be able to accommodate such numbers. At such a point, it wouldn't be just disparity between the haves and the have nots, but worldwide famine would create a situation in which humanitarian aid would be demanded, and could not be ignored.

Through its subsidiaries, the Society has for centuries been able to control and manipulate grain markets, as well as most other food staples. However, world wide food shortages and famines would create panic, and the ability to only sell what is absolutely necessary, would be gone. Seeing the dead and the dying in major cities around the world, would make it absolutely imperative to sell or loan all available grain and food staples, which would destroy the ability to shape and mold the markets as they do at the present time.

While a large scale war might cause the same decrease in population, it would be quite disruptive, and even though the

Society profits from war, it is something they try to avoid. They want to enslave mankind, not eradicate them, and with the technology you have developed over the last half century, another world war would be devastating to their plans. All this to say, that with the research those original scientists had developed, and with further improvements, the Society had the perfect tool with which to eradicate large numbers of people, without any repercussions, or suspicions.

Which brings us back to the oil wars, and the impact it has on society. Much like the grains, or other major commodities, the Society has to a large degree, been able to control the supply of oil to the major countries of the world. However, because there is such an abundance of oil, it was necessary to find a way to curtail the drilling and exploration of new oil fields, and at the same time, keep the development of alternative fuel sources to a minimum.

Since the United States was, and continues to be the largest consumer of oil and oil related products, and since it also has some of the largest deposits of gas, oil and coal, the decision was made to use these resources as a reserve, for years in the future. This does not mean that drilling has stopped, or will stop in the future, but just that large finds, and vigorous production will be stymied. These natural reserves are not being saved for use by the U.S., but for the United Nations. Since technology will not be able to totally replace the many uses of oil for several centuries, it will be critical for this global government to have its own private supply, which will be the reserves in the United States.

Twenty years from now, when foreign oil becomes expensive to the citizens of America, they will demand more use of domestic resources, but members within the government who are sympathetic to the cause of globalization, will refuse to allow these resources to be tapped. This will confuse many people who do not see the logic in not using their own resources, but it is that those resources are being saved, not for them, but the United Nations. Of course, this will not be the reason given for not using these resources, and the twisting of the truth by these immoral politicians, will almost be comical, if it were not such a serious issue.

All this said, because current worldwide production capabilities will outpace demand for many years to come, and it is imperative that the availability of supplies not become so great as to allow what could be called cheap oil, to be had by all countries, but at the same time making sure the U.S. has enough to keep prices at an artificially low level. This will not be easily accomplished, as many variables, such as the value of the dollar, and political instability in the middle east, make manipulation extremely difficult, but for the most part, the next fifteen years will see oil prices fairly steady; between ten and twenty dollars a barrel.

There will be a couple of spikes in price during that time, even dipping below ten dollars as late as 1999, but beginning in 2004, the price will begin to rise to levels not thought possible. With cheap gas no longer available, public outcry from Americans for increased drilling and alternative fuel sources will be the daily cry, but regulations put into place over the last twenty years, along with those of the next fifteen, will make this nearly impossible.

Many of these regulations are, and will continue to be environmentally based, but except for a few exceptions, they will have all been designed to keep the United States from being energy independent. Perhaps the greatest damaging regulation, is the inability to build new refineries. No new refineries have been built since the 1970s, and many are being shut down, and this number will keep declining well into the 2010s. The result of all this is that even when there is oil, many times there will not be enough refineries going to process the oil, causing severe gas shortages and higher prices. During all the years that these regulations are being put into place, only a few individuals will be speaking out against them, but with an apparent abundant supply, the media is able to label these people as extremists, and as a result, no one listens. As mentioned before, this oil has been reserved for the United Nations, and it is by these regulations that it can be kept from being used.

After the fall of the Soviet Union, the United States will be virtually the only super power left in the world, and while there are still countries with strong military armaments, it is the U.S. that is the leader. However, this will not be the case in 2004, and with the emergence of China and other Asian countries as economic powers, the strain put on all available commodities, including oil, will create havoc in some markets.

From the moment the Society decided to try and keep U.S. production to a minimum, and exploit the fields of the middle east, it has known that sooner or later military force might have to be used to maintain some semblance of order in the world oil markets. Thinking that they might be able to forestall such action, they helped form the Organization of Petroleum Exporting Companies, better known as OPEC.

By setting production quotas for each member country, as well as a total for the entire group, world markets would be equitable for all, and all could make plenty of revenue. This arraignment will work fairly well, until two years from now, when two of the original five members have a squabble.

When one of the countries begins stealing oil from the other through a technique called slant drilling, the second country will invade the first, and threaten to take over several other countries in the region, most notably Saudi Arabia, a major ally and supplier in the region to the United States.

This incident will play into the hands of the Society in a variety of ways, and will begin what history will refer to as the oil wars. Not all of these wars and skirmishes will be directly tied to oil, but because they take place in the middle east, it will be necessary to guard the oil fields from those in the area who would seize control over all the fields, and from those countries who might decide to invade for the same reason.

This first war, really skirmish, will be the perfect opportunity to get a military presence in the area, and also to give the United Nations (U.N.) a greater role in the affairs of nations. When the second country complains to the U.N. about the theft of their oil, and that they may have to use military action to rectify the deed, they are given approval to proceed. This was seconded by the same president who not many weeks later, will mention ushering in a new world order, a world where the U.N. would make these type of decisions, and whose authority would not be questioned.

Since the approval to use military action will be insinuated, rather than actually given, there will be no record, and it will be denied that approval was ever given. Nevertheless, within weeks, the first country will be invaded, and immediately steps are going to be taken by the United States, acting through the U.N. to liberate this country from its invaders. Within days, coalition forces began building up in a neighboring country, and just months later, will liberate the invaded country.

Most of the military forces will leave after all peace negotiations have been completed, but enough remain behind in order to insure that the oil fields remain secure, and to give the impression that the United Nations is in control of regional stability.

Over the next decade, this whole region will have regional squabbles, and though there will be reports of mass genocide, the oil fields themselves are relatively secure, so very little concern is given to these rumors.

This will not be the only genocide ignored by the United Nations during this decade, as nearly one million people will be killed in a small African country, in 1994. This inaction by the U.N. only serves to confirm what many have thought all along, that it is solely an organization set up to enslave the nations of the earth, and while this may be factually correct, proving it is nearly impossible.

Too many leaders owe their allegiance to the different groups run by the Society, and since the philosophy of a one world government seems practical to their thinking, they work diligently in globalizing all aspects of life.

During the upcoming decade of the 1990s, China and India, as well as other Asian countries, will increase their economies immensely, and their increasing need for oil will put strains on the market, causing long term financial concerns. There will be a growing concern that one of these countries, or perhaps even Russia, might bring a military presence to the region, in order to secure future supplies, and though talks within the U.N. seem encouraging, behind closed doors there is talk of an imminent attack.

Even though these three countries have a commanding presence in the U.N., it is leaders within the United States and Europe who actually control policy, and are just biding their time until the U.S. citizens have lost all rights, before handing over all governmental operations to U.N. regulations.

With the growing fear that a coalition is forming between

China, Russia and India, these western alliances within the U.N. will begin a campaign of propaganda specifically designed to foster the need to send more troops into the region, when an unexpected, yet opportune event falls into their lap.

This event will be so unexpected, that it will stun the world for several days, but in less than a month, thousands of troops will be sent into the region to capture the man and the group behind this terrorist act, and the oil war will have officially begun.

CHAPTER 16

Not everyone in the world is governed by greed and power, but some men live their lives on principles higher than themselves, and put these principle into practice on a daily basis. These are men who cannot be ruled by other men, nor desire to rule, but at the same time wish to have their principles forced upon others, and such will be the man responsible for this act of terrorism against the United States.

Not long after the turn of the century, there will be a direct attack against the United States, and several thousand people will be killed, many more injured, and though this isn't the first attack made by those responsible, it will be the first attack inside the country itself. This attack will be categorized as a terrorist attack by the United States, a religious war by those perpetrating the act, and for purposes of this chronicle, part of the oil war.

Within a month, a coalition of military forces from around the globe will descend upon the country rumored to be harboring the group responsible for this attack, demanding that they hand over the man who master minded the attacks, and those in his terrorist organization. When the country's ruling government rejects this demand, this coalition of forces, led by American troops, will remove the leaders of that government, and provide for free elections. However, the terrorist organization and its leader will not be destroyed so easily, and the war in this particular country will go on for many years.

This is the opportunity those within the U.N. will have been looking for, and the propaganda campaign begun months earlier, will now have another target in mind to send troops to. By calling these actions a war on terrorism, and seemingly necessary to insure that weapons of mass destruction do not fall into the wrong hands, many more thousands of troops will be sent into the country they had fought just ten years prior to this event, and the leader will be removed from power.

With a large military presence in the area, the U.N. feels secure that the oil fields will be safe from being taken over by either terrorists, or one of the Asian superpowers, and for the most part, the financial markets will reflect this stability. Another benefit is that the terrorist group responsible for the attack on America, and those sympathetic with their cause, will stay in the middle east to fight against these western forces, rather than taking the fight to the cities of the United States, or other major cities in Europe.

A result of all this, is that both these wars will drag on for several years, and just when everyone thinks peace is almost at hand, another major attack will occur. Like the first attack, it will come without warning and in an unsuspecting way. This attack will be biological, and will at first seem to have been caused by faulty equipment at water treatment plants. After six months, investigations will reveal that this was a modified strain of E. coli, that had been generated in a laboratory, and given the necessary properties in which to kill.

Several trial runs will be done in various cities around the world, the first being in a small town in the central U.S., where several hundred people will get sick, but as each test is done, the potency is increased, until the fatality rate is nearly ninety percent. The tests will take several years to complete, but after completion, several major cities in the United States will be infected, and in every case, this bacteria will have been transmitted to the public, by way of the water supply.

During this outbreak, thousands will die, and while this infectious bacteria is short lived, it still takes several months before water supplies become safe again. But this act of terrorism will have left its mark, and people will no longer have confidence that their water supply is in fact back to normal, or that their government can protect them.

Since it will take several months before investigators can determine the exact cause of this outbreak, and even longer before terrorism is confirmed, those responsible will have had time to flee the country, and since no single group claims responsibility, it is unclear who has done it. We watchers who oversee and chronicle all these things, know who will be responsible, but we are forbidden from mentioning names, and the ones responsible will never be caught.

This event will not occur for nearly thirty years, but when it does, and terrorism is blamed, retribution against those thought responsible will be demanded, and yet as horrendous as this act is, it is nothing compared to what is fixing to happen in the middle east and northern Africa.

Thirteen years from now, when the first terrorist attack against the mainland of the United States occurs, there will be many who do not understand why something like this is happening, because it is a type of war that western civilization doesn't understand. Western culture understands going to war for defense, even if that means sometimes committing preemptive strikes, and it also understands defending those nations they have alliances with, it even understands that some countries have desires to conquer others, but it does not understand a war based on philosophical ideals, or religion. The fact that someone might want to eradicate them from off the earth, because of religious beliefs, seems to preposterous.

Yet this is exactly what these terrorists wish to do, and while for the western world this will be a war about oil and national security, for those siding with the terrorist groups, it will be a religious, or holy war.

These terrorists, Muslims of the Islamic religion, view the United States as the great Satan, and seeing the immoral behavior that the U.S. exports throughout the world, deem it necessary to declare a jihad against the United States, and those allied with it. Not all Muslims believe in this jihad, but enough do to keep this war going, which leads to the disaster which will occur in 2025.

Since the Society is over lorded by one of the fallen watchers, it has known that eventually it would have to deal with those whose religious ideologies supersede anything else, and while "pogroms" of the past have been very effective in dealing with the Jews, something more drastic was needed in this case, given the numbers they were dealing with.

In 2008, seeing that the war on terrorism was stagnant, a large influx of U.S. troops will be sent in, a surge if you will, and will be very effective, but only for a short while. A neighboring country whose leaders are committed to bringing about the return of the twelfth Imam, decides to help, even though they were former enemies, and though this help will be less than needed, it does bring new life to the terrorist cause.

It is then, that the Society, working through agencies within the United Nations, will commit the greatest act of genocide ever known in the history of the earth, one in which billions of people will be killed. Knowing that the war was at a stalemate, and could drag on for years, the Society used the technology it had been able to gather from the original AIDS research, and infected close to a half a million people with a deadly strain of a flu virus. These people will in turn infect others, but because this virus will have been developed into a time released virus, it will not take effect for nearly seventeen years.

The way this time release virus works is essentially very

simple, but it will take many years to perfect. By encapsulating this virus in radioactive material, it not only preserves the virus, but when this radioactive material decays, the virus is set loose to do its work. There are many technological workings involved for this virus to be encapsulated, and at the same time having the capacity to spread, but once it is done, it is very easy to transmit it to the intended victims. Most of the infections will be caused through vaccinations, but whether through vaccines or the food supply, no one will ever suspect that this was in fact the means of infecting all these people.

Knowing that such a long time would elapse before this virus would take effect, a vaccine had been prepared beforehand, and most of the western world, and its allies, were inoculated before the infection was released. Those areas most affected by this virus, will be ones in which the predominate religion is Islam, and not only will terrorists be killed, but essentially all Muslims.

At this time, the war, whether it is called the oil war, or the war on terrorism, will essentially be over, and with virtually no people to man these countries, the United Nations will take over these areas for itself, including the large oil reserves that are still left.

This event will essentially bring the world to its knees, and ten years later, when the second phase of the virus takes over, and China and India are decimated, and left with only a few thousand people, it will usher in the new one world order, or government, run by the United Nations, which is in fact the governmental body created by the Society.

The number of people who die in these two pandemics will be in the billions, and the only feasible way to dispose of the bodies, will be to bury them in a valley, a valley designated in times past by the Creator for this very purpose. In both cases it will take nearly seven months to bury them, and those dead who remain unburied, will be eaten by the birds and beasts of the land.

CHAPTER 17

Before moving on and describing more of who and what the Society is, it is necessary to see how the role of religion plays a part in all that is going on. While this will not be in anyway a detailed look at all religions, or even describe in full detail each of their beliefs, it will perhaps enable the reader of this chronicle to see why some seemingly random events, are related. Since there are only three religions which are basically monotheistic, they will be the ones which are obstacles to the Society and its desire to control all mankind.

Other religions tend to be pantheistic, or Unitarian in nature, and have the idea that all religions lead to the same place. While this is incorrect, it tends to be popular with those who are either immoral, and need an excuse for their behavior, or for those who want to deny the great Chronicle given them by the Creator. For others, especially adherents to ancient religions in such places as India, they are not necessarily immoral, but have never known anything else.

Perhaps one of the greatest obstacles in the advancement of

mankind, will be the religion of evolution. Just a theory postulated in the mid 1800s, it soon gained credence among philosophers, and atheists as a way to explain human life, without the existence of the Creator. With no Creator, all things became permissible, or morally indifferent, and this resulted in many of the atrocities seen in the twentieth century.

It also led to the rise of secular humanism, or the belief that man was his own god, and could chart his own destiny, and many of the programs and agendas designed by the United Nations, have this view in mind. But all structures need to have a hierarchy, and those who adhere to the religion of humanism are no different, so there must be an elite class to rule over those not deemed worthy to lead, and to decide what the fate of those people might be. Again, this eventually leads to genocides and tyranny, dispelling the notion that man is basically good.

Evolution in many cases, also leads to the worship of what many people call mother earth. If anything and everything, can trace its beginning back to some primordial soup, then all life, whether plant or animal, must be directly related, and this idea can be seen in many of the actions of those who call themselves environmentalists.

True environmentalism, stewards the earths resources,

using it for the betterment of mankind, but does not place plants and animals on a par with humans. Sadly though, not nearly enough stewardship is going on, and this has resulted in many problems, most of which do not have anything to do with the environment.

Those who practice this earth worship, are also very susceptible and easily swayed to the idea that man causes all problems dealing with the environment. Whether it is the global cooling scare of just a few years ago, or the man made global warming scare that will be coming just over a decade from now, or food shortages, and the list could go on, it is all just a way in which to control the lives of people through fear.

All of these ideas and philosophies seem new, but those who study and understand, know that these are just old religions repackaged for a new consumer, and that there really isn't anything new under the sun. Though these religions sometimes have conflicting views, ones in which if one side is true, the other must be false, the adherents of these false religions seem to agree, against all logic, that they are both true, just going along different paths.

However, the three monotheistic religions, Judaism, Christianity, and Islam, are very dogmatic, and see it very differently. These religions see the world as being created by one God, whom we call the Creator, and that there are certain guidelines on how mankind is to live in relationship to one another, and to the Creator. As a result of these guidelines, it is very hard for a humanistic organization such as the United Nations, to impose its will against these people.

Even now, there are efforts underway to undermine these dogmas, and create an atmosphere where all religions are treated as equally valid, and opposing this validity will be considered not only hateful, but illegal. The right to practice any religion, no matter how erroneous, should be upheld by all, but the right to practice does not automatically validate its truthfulness. Even within the three monotheistic religions, there is a growing acceptance to this theory of unity, and by 2020, there will be very few who adhere strictly to the tenets of their faith.

Those who do stand firm in their beliefs, will be categorized as backward, possibly terrorists, unintelligent, hateful, racist, as well as many other wrongful characteristics, but most of all, they will be considered as those who are hindering the progression of mankind. Speaking out against immoral behavior will be categorized as hate speech, and will be considered an offense worthy of prison.

Religious persecution has always been around, in fact, more people will die in this century for their stand on religion, than in any other previous century, but it will reach a new level in the next century, once the oil war is over, and the United Nations begins its reign. While most of the persecution has been against those who practice Christianity and Judaism, between 2008 and 2025, an increasing number of those persecuted, will be Muslims, and when the great epidemic of 2025 concludes, the Islamic faith will have been eradicated. As mentioned earlier, this epidemic will be as much about ridding the world of Islam, as it is in winning the oil war.

Ironically, one of the Islamic leaders who will be responsible, or at least blamed, for much of the terrorism that occurs during the time of the oil war, will himself revert to Christianity just before he dies, and will convert thousands to this faith. Hunted and hated by the west, for his part in terrorism, and hunted and hated by those of his former faith, for converting, he has little place to hide, yet in spite of all the turmoil he will have caused, he will die peacefully in his sleep during the time of the great epidemic.

Throughout all the war and turmoil that will go on in the middle east, Israel somehow remains unscathed, and even during the great epidemic, very few will die. However, Judaism, will not fare as well, and Israel for the most part will become a secular nation, though in the worlds eyes, it is still Jewish, and will be hated.

Christianity will for all intents and purposes, be the only monotheistic religion left, but the poison of liberalism will have infected their theology to such a degree, that it will be indistinguishable from many of the beliefs that Hindus and Buddhists have. Its effectiveness, or ability to be a changing and commanding force in society will have completely disappeared, and the religion of secular humanism will prevail.

Nevertheless, true Christianity is not dead, and will not remain quiet as to the truth of what is written in the great Chronicle, and the evil being perpetrated on mankind in the guise of socialism, otherwise known as the religion of humanism.

Because religious tolerance will be the law, the intolerance of Christians who say there is only one way, will not be tolerated, and anyone professing the narrow way, will be imprisoned and beheaded. Thousands will be killed at this time, and with the last voice of opposition silenced, the United Nations, the one world government created by the Society to rule over all the affairs of mankind, will reign unhindered.

CHAPTER 18

When the United Nations becomes the global ruling body, and nations are for all practical purposes states, the Society, which controls those in leadership positions, will have little difficulty in finally establishing a single currency. This is something they have been working on for centuries, and now with a single government, its feasibility is more practical, and the transition will be relatively easy.

When the United States currency and economic markets finally collapse in the 2020s, it will take down several other countries with it, and though the United Nations is not yet fully in control, it does have enough viability to have its own currency. Many nations will begin using this currency, and several years later, when the U.N. is fully functional, all countries will be forced to use this one currency.

The transition time to complete all the necessary changes to use this one currency, will only be a matter of months, and for ease of use, it will be cashless. With the technological advances made in the years leading up to this event, physical money will not be necessary, and by being able to monitor all transactions, theft and illegal transactions become almost non existent. It will also make monitoring for tax purposes much easier, and the filing of forms becomes unnecessary, as U.N. agencies automatically do this on a monthly basis.

Everyone, including children, will be given a card, much like a credit card, with personal data, and a personal number, so identity theft is virtually non existent. However, the difficulty in replacing lost cards, and changing names on cards, creates an unforeseen problem, and most people opt to having a computer chip placed in their hand for its ease of use. This cant be lost, and scans as well as the card, and within three years of this cashless society becoming an actuality, all people will be required to receive this chip.

With seemingly no monetary problems, and the world being run by a single government, everything seems to be at peace, for the first time in several thousand years.

No one seems to notice the lack of freedom that exists, and since all the necessities of life, including food and shelter, are provided by the government, those who do see this subjugation, are generally quiet, and go about their daily work. Those very few who do speak out are persuaded in a most compelling manner to desist, and those who don't are imprisoned as enemies of the state, and are never seen or heard from again.

What could be wrong with having a system like this, when everything is at peace? It all comes down to freedom, and the right to choose ones destiny, and free will, and in this system that the Society has created, these are illusions. Freedom, and having the right to choose a certain vocation, or any of a number of different choices in life, brings with it a certain responsibility, including the right to fail. However, those who are enslaved, do not have that choice, and lacking the knowledge that one is enslaved is perhaps worse than failing. It is this enslavement that defines the evil of this Society, and just a few years after everyone is cataloged into the systems of the United Nations, there are going to be some radical changes, but given that peace will exist at this time, most people will go along with the changes. These changes will seem minor when compared with peace and prosperity, so even if there is a form of slavery, can the Society really be called evil?

When the Society announces who they are, and enacts this

final change, they will be hailed as benefactors of mankind, and revered, so who and what is this Society, and what is the final change they will implement?

When one talks about conspiracies, it usually means that some secret action is going on, usually either illegal or immoral, and it is very hard to describe the Society without sounding like their every action is conspiratorial. It is very true, that the Society itself is very secret, and has a very clear cut agenda, but not all of its actions are secretive, and many of the organizations under its leadership are very open in its goals. Some of these groups have many members, and in many respects are not much more than a fraternal organization meeting to discuss the latest topic of the day. Yet, even these groups have ulterior motives in the upper ranks, and if initiates really knew the underlying philosophy behind the organization, they would never join.

This chronicle will mention several of the more prominent groups that perhaps many have heard of, but not a lot of detail will be given on each group. The idea is to give the reader a glimpse of the Society's reach, and how wide spread it is, and while these groups have similar goals, they don't necessarily specialize in the same area of expertise.

Probably the most popular or well known of these lesser

groups, is the freemasons. Many books have been written about this organization, and the various men throughout history who have been a part of this group. Many have been leaders of corporations, some even presidents, but very few in this world wide organization ever reach the upper echelon of membership, and learn its real goal. It is in the upper levels, where some of the ancient secrets are taught, and where members are recruited into other groups.

These other groups have more influence, and tend to be much smaller. Also, the global influence of these smaller groups is much greater. Several of these groups have great influence in various global affairs, and are well known. The Tri-Lateral Commission and the Council on Foreign Relations, better known as the CFR, are just two of the more well known organizations, and much of their work is very public, and those wishing to see what their motives are can easily find publications on their activities.

Other important groups, like the Brookings Institute, and many of the foundations, such as the Carnegie Foundation and Russell Sage Foundation, are less known, but still have important functions in the web of influence.

Some groups have their origins or are directly linked to some of the old, but wealthy European families, one of which has had a member in the Society since ancient times. Whether it is men associating together for a time of relaxation and play at Bohemian Grove, or participating in the secretive Bilderberg meetings, all of them are influential in the governing of the world, and their common ties cannot be ignored.

While not all of these organizations work together, they are linked in one way or another, to some of the ancient assemblies, whose names are rarely heard today. Whether it's the Illuminati, the Council of Thirteen, The Committee of 300, or older more ancient names like The Knights Templar, Serpents of Wisdom, or the Babylonian Brotherhood, they are all gatherings created by the Society, along with numerous others, to work in concert to enslave mankind. The tentacles and interweaving of all the groups that are, or have ever been linked to the Society, are too intricate to describe in such a short chronicle, but it is important to know they are all related to the common goal of placing mankind in chains.

The Society itself, as mentioned earlier, consists of five men, one for each region of the world, and the apprentices who are being mentored to take their place upon their demise. The leader of these five men, the one who teaches them, and oversees their dealings with mankind, is the fallen watcher, the very one who has taught them all, from the beginning.

Not only has this fallen watcher taught these men of the

Society the intricate details of finance and economics, but also how to use these two tools in a concerted way in order to tighten control on all aspects of human life and development. They have also been taught every aspect of the black arts, or occult, things that mankind from the beginning of time has been forbidden to know and practice.

Over the centuries, many of the occult practices have been taught to others, and many of the dark religions seen in the world today, are a direct result of these practices. However, the most powerful, or potent of practices, are only participated in by the five men of the Society, and only with the aid of the fallen watcher. Each of the men stand at a corner of the royal pentagram,(one designed and created specifically for a particular practice,) and the watcher stands at the center, and speaks what must be spoken. This particular event has only been used perhaps half a dozen times in the history of mankind, and to give any more details than this, has been strictly forbidden. This is only mentioned, for at the time when the United Nations becomes fully functional, this distinct act will be performed once more.

It is also at this time, that the Society will reveal themselves to the world, and explain how they have been working on this centuries long solution to world peace, and that the prosperity and peace of this new world order can all be ascribed to one benefactor, and that is when the fallen watcher will be revealed as this benefactor.

In turn, this fallen watcher, who must remain nameless, will be rewarded by being given the highest title available, that of Secretary General of the United Nations. Through centuries of deceit and treachery, this watcher has finally enslaved mankind, and become its leader, and within days, will make his one, and essentially last decree.

This decree will state, that while he has been overseer throughout the centuries in causing this great peace and prosperity come to pass, it has actually been the light bearer, that fallen angel better known as Lucifer, who has been the earths protector and benefactor, and worship is to be ascribed to him. By describing him as the light bearer, or rather the one who has brought enlightenment and intellectualism into the world, men worship him as a god, and as there are no believers in the true Creator to discredit this claim, all men, great and small, women and children, worship this being, and choose him as the supreme being over all mankind.

The new world order has in fact become a reality, with a seemingly benevolent ruler, and peace and prosperity flourish, and this one who has given it to them, the one who has hated and desired the enslavement of mankind since the beginning, is worshipped as he had hoped. However, everything is not well, for the Creator has put it into men's hearts to be of one mind, giving their kingdom and worship to this evil one, and soon it will all begin to unravel, at which time the fate of man becomes grim.

CHAPTER 19

This chronicle has presented a very bleak future for the next forty years, and while most of it has focused on events which will happen in the United States, it encompasses all of mankind. Since the United States is the last real obstacle in the realization of the coming New World Order, its fate is especially important.

Also, because of the nature of this chronicle, many of the subjects could not be explained but in the most brevity of manner, sometimes leaving more questions than answers.

However, this chronicle was written in order that enough people might heed what is going to occur, and if possible, change the course of history. The chance of this happening is almost non-existent, for the forces that have been working for centuries, are very powerful, and will not allow resistance to succeed, and though possible, very unlikely. Though this is a pertinent reason, the most important reason this chronicle was written is to be a witness against those individuals who, knowing what is going to happen, not only allow it, but refuse to even become involved in resisting it.

In order to change the course of history, several new paradigm shifts in thinking must occur. First, a thirst for the knowledge and wisdom of truth for its own sake must take place. Not for the motive of getting a better job, or more money, but solely for the truth and freedom it brings to all. Secondly, there must be an innate desire to see the advancement of all mankind, with no ulterior motive. This means friend helping friend, neighbor helping neighbor, and families helping families, but of utmost importance, it must be on a personal level.

It has never been, nor ever will be, the governments right or responsibility to replace the charitable duty of all its citizens, and when it does, it ends up practicing thievery. Lastly, it is imperative that there is a return to the morality given by the Creator to mankind. This not only demonstrates self dignity, but reveals that each individual has dignity, and this right cannot or should not be taken away. It is essential that these three practices be put into place, not only because it is right, but change will be useless without them.

Human nature being what it is, and the power these forces you will be up against have, it is very unlikely this change will come, but if you can get past that time in the early part of the next century without the United States being attacked, many of the events foretold in this chronicle, will not come to pass.

Know this though, that if change does not occur, you will go through these events, and mankind will be enslaved by an all encompassing world government, a New World Order led by a being you will be compelled to worship.

Do not fret about what you cannot change, and do not think that it is the end of mankind, for the Great Chronicle reveals a future beyond this, but that will be for another time, another watcher, and another chronicle.

So ends the Chronicle of T'Narg.